The Last Heartbeat:
A Husband's Final Gift

Divina Blanco

Ukiyoto Publishing

All global publishing rights are held by

Ukiyoto Publishing

Published in 2025

Content Copyright © Divina Blanco

ISBN 9789370098459

All rights reserved.
No part of this publication may be reproduced, transmitted, or stored in a retrieval system, in any form by any means, electronic, mechanical, photocopying, recording or otherwise, without the prior permission of the publisher.

The moral rights of the author have been asserted.

This book is sold subject to the condition that it shall not by way of trade or otherwise, be lent, resold, hired out or otherwise circulated, without the publisher's prior consent, in any form of binding or cover other than that in which it is published.

www.ukiyoto.com

Dedication

To my husband, Bhanupong

Acknowledgement

I wish to thank the following people who supported me throughout the writing of this book:

My editors: Normita Thongtham and Wadee Deeprawat

My friends and relatives who gave me light during the darkest moments of my life, Barbara May Contreras Mauhay, Brenda Calida-Buktaw, Zenaida Vannaying, Alisa "Betty" Phongsathorn, Lucia Sukhanenya, Wantana Suchaviva, Aong-orn "Apple" Somprasong, Chutiporn "Judy" Chombhubol, Vipawat Misitsakul, Cynthia Ortiz-Gorry, Yolanda Hernandez, Rosemarie Raymundo, Marie Jean Jorge Ohara, Teresita Jovellano -King and the ICC'73 batchmates, Dr. Naris Chaiyasoot, Maria Socorro "Corina" Gochoco-Bautista, Suresh and Lyn Narayanan, Leila Marie Gonzales, Anton Mercurio, my brother, Cicero " Chito " and Janette Blanco and the Stella Maris Seafarers Mission Center family.

Contents

Prologue	1
Chapter One November-December: A Season of Despair	6
Chapter Two January: A Promise of Hope	69
Chapter Three February: A Time of Persistence	85
Chapter Four March: Shattered Hope	103
Chapter Five April: The Descent of Twilight	132
Chapter Six May: Journey to the Stars	151
About the Author	*178*

Prologue

"Because I could not stop for Death -
He kindly stopped for me -
The Carriage held but just Ourselves -
And Immortality."
- Emily Dickinson, "Because I Could Not Stop for Death"

A Dream of Cherries

Morning. Sunshine streams through my windowpane, casting a golden glow across the room. The air hums with city life - honking cars, hammering construction workers, bursts of laughter, and sharp curses. Children's laughter reverberates from a nearby playground, a melody of innocence.

For a fleeting moment, I can almost hear, "Breakfast is ready!", the creak of my bedroom door, and a much-loved face peeping in.

But the door stays shut. There's only silence.

That face, I now see only in dreams. Like last night.

It must have been our first summer as international students in Baltimore, Bhanu and I. Summers there, our home for the next five years, felt like a daily adventure.

The streets simmered under the relentless sun, the air thick and sticky. I was returning home on the bus from Towson University, where I had just finished my summer classes. It was noon, the sun directly overhead. Sweat clung to my skin, and my hair was damp. The sparse breeze stirred by the unairconditioned bus offered no relief from the oppressive heat, made worse by impatient passengers yearning for somewhere cooler.

Beside me, a teenager in a white spaghetti-strap blouse fidgeted restlessly, her armpits dripping with perspiration. I ignored her, captivated by the passing scenery of tree-lined streets and stately homes that slowly receded from view.

As we neared the city limits, the fresh scent of trees gradually gave way to Baltimore's signature mix of exhaust fumes and summer fruits. The bus crawled to the intersection of Greenmount and 33rd Street, a familiar intersection woven into our story. There, I spotted Bhanu.

From afar, I could see him pacing anxiously around a crowded bus stop shelter. He stood out in his two-toned blue button-down shirt, long black pants, and leather shoes - an incongruous figure amidst a sea of summer attire: cotton T-shirts and baggy shorts for men, and spaghetti straps and short shorts for women. He brushed a stray strand of hair from his face, evidence of my fumbling attempts at haircutting. Beads of sweat glistened on his youthful face and slim build under the harsh midday sun.

The bus shuddered to a stop and the doors hissed open. I lunged for the exit, jostling past other passengers like a frantic animal escaping a cage. When Bhanu saw me rushing towards him, his face lit up with a radiant smile. His eyes twinkled as he waved his left hand, then pointed excitedly with his index finger to a bag he held in his right hand - a bag overflowing with plump, red cherries, my favorite fruit.

At the sight of the cherries, I quickened my pace. Bhanu hurried to meet me, but suddenly a large, faceless man, his sunburnt skin slick with sweat, barreled into him. The impact sent Bhanu sprawling, the bag of cherries flying into the air in a crimson explosion.

Like a sprinter in a race, I bolted towards Bhanu to help him gather the scattered fruit. But in a scene ripped from a horror movie, the spot where I had last seen him was now deserted and eerily quiet. There was no sign of him, no evidence he had ever been there, except for the crushed cherries, their red juice staining the pavement like blood from a wound. Bhanu had vanished, seemingly swallowed whole by the blinding midday sun.

My heart hammered in my chest, a frantic drumbeat of disbelief, shock, and terror. It pounded like a muffled bell underwater, its sound lost in the oppressive silence. I tried to call out his name, but to my horror, I was voiceless. My throat constricted, searching for a sound that would not come. A strangled sob died in my throat as I sank to my knees, hot tears streaming down my face.

My trembling fingers brushed the cherry bag, expecting nothing. Instead, I felt something soft and familiar beneath my fingertips.

Gasping, my eyes fluttered open. My vision was blurry, my head foggy. I was not sprawled on a hot sidewalk amidst scattered cherries. Cradling my soft pillow, I was lying in the cool darkness of our bedroom, the air conditioner humming softly. A heavy stillness, thick with memories, hung in the air, amplifying the emptiness in my heart.

Outside, the pre-dawn silence shattered with the clinking and clunking of garbage collectors emptying trash cans. As their sounds faded into the distance, only the muffled echo of my own heartbeat remained.

The soft glow of the bedside clock displayed the time: 2:00 a.m. It was the hour Bhanu would usually emerge from his study after a night of writing, research, and grading papers.

My hand instinctively reached out to the other side of the bed, a habitual gesture ingrained in the rhythm of countless nights. My fingers met only cold sheets, the hollowness mirroring the void within me. Bhanu's two pillows, adorned in shades of blue - his favorite color, coincidentally mine as well - lay there expectantly. One a solid, calming blue, the other patterned with delicate baby blue roses.

Those pillows, which I meticulously arranged every night, seemed to hold the essence of his presence. They awaited the weight of his head, the imprint of his dreams, and the warmth of his body nestled between them.

Tonight, and for the last several months, the pillows stood witness to an absence, leaving behind the sad echo of what used to be.

Sleep was impossible. My mind spun in the dark, tangled with memories and the sound of the night.

Now, it is morning. Another day of waiting for something that will never happen.

Footsteps reverberate outside our front door. I sit up, heart lifting, half-expecting to hear Bhanu's key turning the lock and his hurried steps crossing the threshold. His arms wrapping around me, his face breaking into that broad, familiar smile.

But the footsteps fade down the hallway, like a tide receding from the shore.

The sound ebbs, leaving only silence.

Leaving only me. Alone.

Two years earlier, I was alone, too. Waiting for Bhanu to come home.

Chapter One
November-December: A Season of Despair

"Behold, we know not anything,
I can but trust that good shall fall,
And last, far off—at last, to all.
And every winter change to spring."

-Alfred, Lord Tennyson, *"In Memoriam, A.H. H., Canto LIV"*

Poinsettias in Gloom

That day clings to my mind like a stubborn morning mist, resisting even the sun's fiercest rays, its drops clinging in every recess of memory. It was the last Tuesday of November - a day seemingly ordinary yet destined to engrave itself indelibly into my memory. The morning began like any other: the air was crisp, the sun bright, and the sky a clear expanse of blue.

"Another warm day," I thought, as I glanced around our cozy living room.

Scarlet and yellow silk poinsettias adorned the table, their vibrant hues whispering of Christmas traditions and the festive season fast approaching. They waited to be hung on the tree Bhanu and I had planned to decorate that weekend.

Bhanu had even promised to bring home real poinsettias if he could spare a moment between his online meetings - or muster the energy to visit the plant shop a few kilometers away.

Yet, beneath the festive anticipation, an undercurrent of unease persisted. For two weeks, Bhanu had battled relentless nausea, a shadow that refused to lift. At first, we attributed it to the antiviral medication we had both taken three weeks earlier after succumbing to Covid-19. My symptoms vanished after the prescribed five days, but Bhanu's worsened with each passing day.

He had isolated himself in our spare room to let me sleep undisturbed, and as a precaution after catching the virus later than me. Yet, I could still hear his frequent visits to the bathroom, each trip a reminder of his struggle. Last night was the worst. He could hardly sleep or eat, leaving him drained and weak.

This morning, despite his weakened condition, he whipped his favorite frittata, his attempt at normalcy.

"I have decided to go to Samitivej this morning," he said, referring to a private hospital a mere ten minutes from our place. It seemed nobody could tell him the cause of his debilitating nausea.

"I need to figure out this digestion nightmare," he continued. His frustration hung heavy as he cancelled an online meeting. He rose, leaving the untouched frittata like a deflated sun on the table.

"You haven't eaten anything," I said, concerned.

"That's okay. I'll grab something in the hospital," he replied as he prepared to leave, wearing his favorite navy-blue cotton shirt like a security blanket protecting him from bad things along his way. It hung a little loosely than before as he tightened his belt to keep his black pants from slipping.

As he walked toward the door, he gently squeezed my arm, smiling wanly. Each step seemed deliberate, as though he carried an invisible weight. For unknown reasons, I suddenly felt uneasy, a premonition of darkness on the horizon.

For most of the morning, I paced the length of the living room, its familiar comfort offering no solace. My eyes were glued to the clock, waiting for Bhanu's return from Samitivej. The bright hues of the poinsettias mocked my growing unease, their festive cheer failed to dispel the fear gnawing at me.

As the hours stretched on without a word from Bhanu, I became more worried. Then my phone buzzed, breaking my gloom. It was the message I had been waiting for all year: my publisher announcing that my first children's book was about to be published, initially as an electronic book, then in a few weeks, as a hard copy.

"I'm published! A childhood dream come true!" I screamed silently.

But within seconds, my joy plummeted. This achievement, earned with Bhanu's unwavering support, felt hollow without him beside me to share it.

He was the only person who believed in me; in what I could achieve. He was the one who encouraged me to write. He was my number one cheerleader, to get me going and to continue writing when I felt I had nothing to write. He was my first editor, giving me suggestions on how to improve the story.

Most of all, he was always there, keeping my spirits up when I felt down.

But he was not here with me now. He was in a hospital anxiously waiting for his fate.

Time crawled on, inching to early afternoon. My feeling of euphoria was interspersed with inexplicable foreboding.

Finally, the front door opened. Bhanu walked in, his voice was like a pilot's monotone announcing turbulence, calm but laced with raw anxiety.

"It's stage four liver cancer," he said, the words landing with the force of a wrecking ball.

I froze unbelieving, staring at his face. His eyes were wide like a deer caught in the headlights of a fast-approaching car, darting left, then right, seeking refuge in the middle of a storm.

Finally, his gaze settled on me, on my walking stick. Then with an unsteady voice, he said, "This is so unfair. I am supposed to take care of you always."

Quickly, he looked away. Perhaps to avoid looking at me, fearing that I might cry. Or, maybe afraid I would see through his eyes how he felt.

I was glued to my chair. Numb. I did not know what to think; or what to say. "No! This can't be true!"

My heart ached for his comforting lie, for a boisterous "I got you, didn't I? Everything is fine. It's just the side effect of the antiviral medicine as we have suspected."

Then we would erupt in laughter, the sound chasing away the ghosts of fear. His mischievous eyes twinkling delightfully for scaring the daylight out of me. This was just another play, our daily dance of harmless pranks and near-heart attacks.

But the silence lingered, heavy and frightening.

Moments later, I heard him say, "I have to see my primary oncologist for further tests at Siriraj Hospital, darling." His words, brittle and clinical, broke the silence. His voice echoed with resignation, bringing me back to reality.

The room became a blur of movements as Bhanu rushed from one room to another, looking for things he would bring to the hospital, his mobile phone, a notebook, and a pen. He hastily threw a few clothes into his overnight backpack. It was now past three in the afternoon. He had to be at Siriraj before 5 p.m. to schedule an emergency CT scan and more tests the next day.

"Let me help you," I said, finally finding my voice. My hands touched his, clumsy against his shaking fingertips.

"Don't pack too many clothes. I will be back tomorrow for sure," his voice was steady but strained.

"We don't know that," I said, trying to sound in control.

"You worry too much," he said, trying to calm me, a forced smile on his lips.

"What exactly did the doctor at Samitivej say?" finally the words heavy with unspoken fear sputtered out of my mouth.

He hesitated and, for a moment, looked away. Then his gaze met mine with silent apology. Reluctantly he gave me Samitivej's medical report, a thin sheath of paper that felt heavy with dreaded truths.

My throat tightened, and my heart raced as my eyes scanned the report that felt as menacing as a cobra's fangs about to bite and spread its deadly venom.

General Appearance: *looked weak, mildly pale, mildly jaundiced, no pitting edema, no signs of chronic liver disease.*

Abdomen: *normal contour, no abdominal distension, soft, not tender, suspected hard mass at the epigastric area, size about 3-4 cm, the liver just palpable, spleen not palpable, no ascites noted.*

So far, nothing seemed extraordinarily serious.

But then:

PROVISIONAL DIAGNOSIS:

- Painless progressive jaundice with ill-defined epigastrial mass, significant weight loss

Very high Carbohydrate Antigen (CA-- a liver/pancreatic cancer indicator***) 19-9 level-, 82,416.50 U/ml (Normal: 0-37 U/ml).***

The numbers screamed, **Code red! Code red!**

I closed my eyes for a moment, hoping and praying that when I opened them again, the report would say something else. Anything else. But the terrifying numbers were still there, followed by:

R/O PANCREATIC CANCER (*Rule Out pancreatic cancer, more tests needed*)

I shivered. My thoughts spiraled. Which is worse: liver or pancreatic cancer? I did not know. I just knew both were devastating.

This can't be true! Wasn't it just eight days ago that he had a stomach ultrasound at a government cancer hospital?

I remembered the report clearly:

Liver: *normal size, shape, and parenchymal echo. No space-occupying lesion is identified.*

The visualized pancreas and spleen are unremarkable.

Then on November 25, he had a chest X-ray in the same hospital with the following findings:

Lungs: *no abnormal pulmonary opacity*

Heart: *normal size*

Abdomen: *unremarkable bony structures and upper abdomen*

None of it prepared me for this.

"I have to go now," Bhanu said gently, his soft voice cutting through the storm in my head.

I looked up, the poisonous medical report fluttering from my shaky hand. Then my eyes met a face I barely recognized.

His lips, which usually curved into an easy smile, were now drawn tight with worry. His eyes, which often sparkled with mischief, now held a depth of fear I had never seen before. And yet beneath it, a flicker of courage.

I swallowed hard, forcing my voice to steady. "Take care. Drive carefully," I said, sounding strangely too calm, too composed.

As he walked to the door, he lowered the brim of his black Mercedes Benz baseball cap, covering his downcast eyes. He hugged me briefly but avoided looking directly into my eyes. The words seemed to catch in his throat as he said, "I'll call you later," his voice hardly audible.

I stood frozen. I was unable to open my mouth, fearing that if I said something more, I would break down as I watched him gently close the door.

As I listened to the sound of his receding footsteps, I wanted so much to run after him, to say something encouraging. But I just stood paralyzed, still shocked at the events of the day.

Denial

My mind and my heart still refused to believe the hospital report; that our lives have suddenly become horrifyingly uncertain. "None of it was true," I wanted to shout. After all, the world outside seemed normal, nothing had changed.

It was the usual Bangkok afternoon rush hour. The streets were jammed with heavy traffic, filled with the cacophony of vehicles honking impatiently. At the same time, the angry noise was drowned by happy laughter of children playing at a nearby playground.

Everything felt surreal. It was as if I were watching a movie about our life, a film that began beautifully but then abruptly shifted into a scene with a poorly written script.

I clung to the belief that we could rewrite this part, that we could rewrite the script. Soon, everything would be back to normal. Bhanu could not be that sick. The test results must be erroneous.

"There must be a mistake. I'm sure it's a mistake," I told myself adamantly, refusing to accept the diagnosis.

"Surely, the tests tomorrow will reveal these numbers to be wrong. The equipment could be faulty. Didn't the preliminary diagnosis mentioned rule out pancreatic cancer? Perhaps the tests will show that it is just a case of severe jaundice.

"Perhaps he will recover within a few months. Just like his stage four prostate cancer diagnosis two years ago, which had miraculously gone into remission a year later after radiation and hormone therapies."

The possibility of another miracle comforted me.

This feeling was reinforced by his messages later that evening. They arrived like lifelines, a delicate exchange of reassurance and mundane details that masked the gravity of his situation.

"Are you okay? I am worried about you all alone," he wrote, attempting to downplay the severity of his condition.

"Don't worry. I will manage," I replied. "How are you? Have you had dinner?" I asked.

"I'm fine. I had fish for dinner," he replied. "How was yours?"

"I had bread with the pasta sauce you cooked yesterday," I replied. Our exchange was like finding shelter amidst a storm blowing our life.

He responded with a sticker of a bear in bed sending a goodnight kiss, bringing cheer to my solitary night.

Early the next day, before the sun was up, Bhanu was already preparing for another test, a CT scan. His call broke the early morning silence.

"Did you sleep well?" he asked.

"Not really. I miss my teddy bear," I replied, still trying to calm my nerves from a troubled sleep.

"The scan showed a lump in my pancreas but the liver seemed all right," he reported later.

"The tumor has blocked my bile duct," he continued. "It is the main cause of my nausea, loss of appetite, and jaundice. The doctors will insert a metal stent so the bile can continue to flow to the small intestine and assist digestion."

It sounded complicated and disheartening. "I hope the procedure won't be painful," I messaged back.

"I don't know but that means I will be here for another night. I miss you," his message said.

I wanted to say I did not like spending the night without him either but I did not want to worry him unnecessarily.

"I miss ambushing my helpless teddy bear especially when he just came out of the shower," my message injected a lighter note.

"Naughty girl!" he replied. "You probably ate a Japanese hostage this morning." His message was a reference to me mishearing Japanese sausage as Japanese hostage. He used it regularly to tease me that I was getting old and hard of hearing.

"By the way, I forgot to tell you that I bought a bag of peanuts the other day. It is in the fridge," he added, a subtle touch of thoughtfulness.

"Thank you for the peanuts," I answered, moved by the thought that despite feeling unwell four days ago, he found the strength to go to the supermarket and buy my favorite stuff, like peanuts.

"I wonder about your meals when I'm not around to cook. Do you have enough food and other household supplies?" he inquired.

"I'm fine. Don't worry about me. It is your health that I'm very concerned about," I replied.

"Let's not talk about it, shall we? I would like us to have a good rest," he replied, changing the topic.

"Here's your favorite sticker, Mr. Bear kissing Lady Bear. Just imagine I'm Mr. Bear and you, of course, are Lady Bear," he said, a tender moment amid the gloom.

"Here's Lady Bear, jumping on your back," I messaged back, continuing the playful banter.

"No wonder my back hurts. You are too heavy," he joked. "Yikes, I haven't showered for two days now," he added, revealing the depth of his discomfort.

"You must stink!" I teased, providing a lighter moment.

"I will shower now. Please eat well. If you run out of food, just order delivery," he said, his voice filled with worry.

"I'll call you later after the stent has been implanted," he added, bringing us back to reality.

Evening came. His messages continued to be a blend of sweetness and concern over daily things.

"Mr. Brown kisses Lady Bear. He missed her the whole day," he sent a sweet sticker again.

"How are you? Have you eaten yet?" I messaged back.

"Yes. I had two spoons of rice, chicken soup, and a banana," he replied.

"That's all? You have to eat more," I said.

"No appetite. I'm still nauseous," he replied. "How about you? Please eat well."

"Don't worry about me. I'm okay," I replied, thinking how hungry Bhanu must be. But he never complained about his hunger pangs.

He used to love eating dinner. Often, we would go to a neighborhood Italian restaurant. He would let me order for him. He loved *spaghetti alle vongole*.

"Let's have Italian dinner when I come home. I haven't taken you out to dinner for so long already," he texted.

"It's perfectly okay with me. What matters most is for you to gain weight and be strong again. You have lost a lot of weight. I'm worried," I texted back.

"Let's not talk about depressing things," he reminded me.

"Do you still have your blood pressure medicine?" he asked, changing the subject. "I'll order for you as soon as I return home."

"Good night, sleep tight. Don't let the bed bug bite," I texted, trying to sound funny.

"I will see you in my dreams," he replied.

He did not call the following morning. Instead, he sent a text. Perhaps he did not want me to hear the fear and hopelessness in his voice. Or maybe he was afraid I might cry when I heard the news, and that would devastate him even more.

So, he texted the following clinical yet deeply chilling message:

"Pancreatic cancer confirmed. It has spread to my tenth rib and very close to my liver. My oncologist recommended I have chemotherapy before the end of December to slow down the spread of the cancer."

He added: "Prognosis: I have three months to three years to live, depending on how my body responds to the treatment."

I stared at the screen, reading the messages over and over again.

Three months... three years. A countdown I hadn't known had already begun.

I did not cry nor scream. I just sat there, suspended. My mind went blank, my body weightless and heavy all at once.

I felt the world crash beneath me. But I was still standing, somehow.

A sudden chill swept through the room, or maybe it was just inside me. My throat felt dry; I couldn't swallow. I wasn't sure I was breathing.

Our life story had shifted in a single moment, tilting towards a frightening, uncertain future. I was left in that awful stillness-- knowing everything had changed, yet having no idea what to do in the days ahead.

Seeking refuge, my mind -- unwilling to stay in that bleak stillness - darted toward its now familiar escape hatch: denial.

I searched for comfort the way I would reach for a light switch in the dark. Once again, I shut off the brutal news. Didn't Bhanu always quote the lines from Robert Browning's poem "Rabbi Ben Ezra" on my birthdays? *"Grow old along with me! The best is yet to be..."*

He would write those words full of certainty on my birthday card every year. We both believed in them - not just as poetry, but as a pact. A promise we never thought would break.

So, we both clung to that promise. Stubbornly. Naively. As if words could ward off fate. As if love alone could rewrite prognosis.

We chose, again, not to look too closely at the ominous signs. We had been here before. A different diagnosis. A different terror. But the same desperate hope.

Journey to Hades – Prostate Cancer

It all started in October 2020, when the world was still in the clutches of the devastating Covid-19 pandemic, a horrific force that afflicted the world since the beginning of the year. Fear hung in the air like a thick fog, with the threat of infection looming over every soul.

As the daily death toll became an agonizing obsession, the world witnessed an unprecedented cascade of measures to stem the tide of widespread virus. Countries sealed their borders; sports events were cancelled; schools closed; employees worked from home; people started wearing masks and observed social distancing; and economic activities were at a standstill.

Despite these draconian measures, the virus was still spreading rapidly and the death toll was rising exponentially. Hospitals were overwhelmed and health systems in most countries were close to breaking down. People were losing their jobs, and many were becoming destitute, desperate, hungry, and hopeless. Fear was stalking everyone.

While the world struggled with this collective trauma, at home we were dealing with an unsettling health problem of our own.

Usually, a sound sleeper, Bhanu had been waking up frequently in the middle of the night these last couple of months.

"Again?" I asked anxiously when Bhanu returned to bed after another trip to the bathroom. "How many times already since we went to bed?

"Three times," he said, drawing a sigh as he changed his shirt.

I glanced at the bedside clock. It was three in the morning. We went to bed at eleven after watching a movie. Three times in four hours. My throat turned dry.

"I'm sorry, darling, for waking you up," he said apologetically, holding my hand.

"That is all right. You know I am a very light sleeper, especially when my teddy bear moves," I replied, squeezing his outstretched hand.

After a few minutes, Bhanu fell asleep. Listening to his breathing, I lay awake, unable to go back to sleep. My mind was full of disturbing thoughts. I remembered the dream I had the other night.

In my dream, Bhanu and I were sleeping in a bed with white sheets and white pillowcases. For some strange reason, our bed was in the basement of a house on a river bank. The river, dark and murky, mirrored the unsettling reality encroaching upon our lives. Massive black ants, like an omen of impending doom, climbed over each other, relentlessly advancing toward us.

I frantically tried to wake Bhanu but I lost my voice. Desperate, I shook him hard, but he continued sleeping as the ants overtook us. Frozen in fear as one ant bit me, I let out a silent scream. Then, I woke up in a cold sweat, realizing it was just a dream.

In the darkness, sleep was now impossible as I watched the entrancing dance of shadows cast by the city lights outside, playing like ethereal puppets on our bedroom curtain. But the images failed to ease the scary thoughts crowding my mind.

My fear increased when I, instinctively, touched Bhanu's back. He was soaked in night sweat, a frightening indication of an underlying condition. Worried, I quickly but quietly got up to get him a new nightshirt.

"What are you doing?" Bhanu asked, annoyed.

"I got you a new shirt. You are soaking wet," I replied with an unusual calm.

"Darling, you shouldn't have. You should be sleeping by now," he admonished. "You know very well that you have to sleep eight hours every night. Doctor's order, remember?"

"I'm just worried about you," I confessed.

"Stop worrying. I am going to see my urologist in two days. Now, let's get some sleep. Please don't get up early. I'll get you freshly baked bread in the morning," he said.

His words were a balm to my troubled soul.

"Okay, okay," I replied, feeling reassured that Bhanu would be consulting his doctor soon, and perhaps find answers to his bladder problem and night sweats. In the predawn hours, our worries retreated momentarily as we finally fell into a deep, restful sleep.

"I'm leaving early," Bhanu said after lunch on the day of his appointment. "My appointment with the urologist is at 4 p.m. but they have scheduled a Covid test before I see the doctor.

"And have dinner without me, just in case I will be late. I have already prepared your meal. Just heat it up."

Listening to him, his voice seemingly unconcerned, it was difficult to tell whether Bhanu was worried about his health.

As the clock ticked away, we filled the time in the most modern of ways -- through text messages and calls. Bhanu, in an attempt to lighten the mood, shared jokes, providing a momentary respite from the boredom of waiting. The laughter echoed through digital channels, keeping us both temporarily cheerful in the face of uncertainty.

Bhanu (17:00): "Still waiting for my turn. Here's something for you while waiting for me. Forwarding a religious joke."

Our digital exchanges continued as the hours dragged on, until Bhanu finally shared a disturbing update.

Bhanu (19:30): "Test finished two hours ago. Met the doctor. I am on my way home."

Me: "How was it?"

Bhanu: "I will tell you when I get home."

Me: "I don't like the sound of it."

Bhanu responded with wisdom, quoting, "Nurture strength of spirit to shield you in sudden misfortune.

But do not distress yourself with dark imaginings. Many fears are born of fatigue and loneliness," from *Desiderata*.

His attempt to soothe my worries brought a momentary comfort, but a lingering unease persisted.

At 9 p.m., the atmosphere turned foreboding as Bhanu arrived home, his face inscrutable.

"It's not good," he said quietly, and a chill swept through the room. It was not the cold that caused my shiver; it was the weight of those words.

"My Gleason score is 9," he continued, his voice steady as he removed his shoes. I rushed to his side, and he squeezed my hand.

"I will have more tests to determine the stage of my cancer and the appropriate treatment," he continued as heaviness suddenly settled in our room.

"What else did the doctor say?" my voice was a mixture of anxiety and impatience.

"He said if it has not spread yet, it can be treated to prevent it from spreading. There are many options. We will know next month after my CT scan," he reassured, but his eyes betrayed a deeper truth.

Behind the words, there was an understandable deep worry. His gaze locked onto mine with an intensity that spoke volumes, revealing the unspoken fear we both felt.

That night, as Bhanu slept beside me, I lay awake staring at the ceiling. My mind raced through all the possibilities, from the most hopeful to the direst. I found myself bargaining with whatever forces might be listening -- I would give anything, everything, if only he could be well again.

Days passed in a blur as December finally arrived, bringing with it a mixture of anticipation and dread.

Then came the results -- Bhanu's CT scan confirmed our worst fear: Bhanu's cancer had advanced to stage 4 with a miniscule tumor detected in his right pelvic bone. The news struck like a bombshell, shattering our fragile optimism that we were still in the early stages of the fight.

Although the holidays were fast approaching promising a time of joy and togetherness, there was no time to delay. Bhanu's doctor swiftly prescribed an aggressive course of treatment: an 18-month hormone therapy commencing on December 29, 2020, and 28 consecutive days of radiation therapy beginning on January 26, 2021, weekends excepted.

The final session was set for March 9, 2021 -- a date that seemed both far away and impossibly close.

The treatment laid before us was like a roadmap through Hades -- dark, uncertain, and frightening. But at least it was a path forward, and we would walk it together, one day at a time.

Life under the threat of Damocles' Sword

Amid the grim diagnosis, Bhanu's oncologist remained steadfastly optimistic. At 66 years old,

Bhanu had much in his favor: a healthy weight, normal blood sugar, cholesterol and blood pressure levels, as well as excellent liver and kidney function.

His disciplined lifestyle -- no smoking or drinking, regular exercise, and balanced meals -- bolstered the doctor's confidence that Bhanu could overcome this challenge. For a time, we allowed ourselves to believe in this possibility, daring to hope that he could still live to a ripe old age.

But as the treatments began, new challenges emerged, testing Bhanu's resilience and our shared strength. The preparation for each radiation session became a daily ordeal.

Bhanu had to endure the discomfort of a painfully full bladder to ensure accurate targeting of the cancerous cells. "Drink lots of water. Your bladder must be full," the nurse instructed, her tone matter-of-fact.

"I want to pee! God, I can hardly hold my pee," Bhanu muttered, his face contorted in discomfort as he lay on the treatment table for what felt like an eternity.

The radiation beams worked silently, targeting the enemy within, while Bhanu waged his own private battle against the demands of the treatment.

The side effects began subtly but soon escalated. Nausea plagued him, and meals became a minefield. Foods that once brought him comfort now betrayed him.

"I think I should not eat sourdough anymore," he said one morning, his tone tinged with frustration.

"Why? It's supposed to be healthier than white bread," I replied, eager to find a solution.

"It's probably the one giving me stomach gas," he guessed.

We tried oatmeal, but it did not help. Soft-boiled rice failed, too. Even tomatoes, once a staple of his diet, caused problems.

The list of forbidden foods grew longer, and as his options dwindled, so did his weight. Each bite became a calculated risk, a small battle in an unending war.

As nausea persisted, new symptoms emerged. His rectum became inflamed, leading to bouts of heavy bleeding and searing pain.

Yet Bhanu bore it all in stoic silence, hiding his suffering from me. He woke up earlier than usual, using the quiet hours of the morning to walk longer distances, as if trying to outpace his illness and shield me from the reality of his struggle.

"Where are you going? It's still very early," I asked one morning, half-awake.

"Sorry, I didn't mean to wake you. Go back to sleep," he replied gently. "I'd like to get my walk early."

Over breakfast, he finally confessed, his voice calm but tinged with worry. "I had heavy rectal bleeding this morning. I'll go to the hospital tomorrow to see my doctor. I'll probably need a colonoscopy."

My heart sank. "Oh my God! Was it painful?" I asked, my voice trembling. Both of us feared colon cancer.

He noticed my distress and downplayed his suffering. "A little," he said with a faint smile. "Please don't worry. I don't like it when you're stressed. It's bad for your blood pressure. It would be terrible if both of us were sick."

The following day, he returned from his appointment with a big smile. "The rectal bleeding was just a side effect of radiation. No colonoscopy for now. And the best news is that my PSA is now down to 0.018!"

Relief washed over me. "Guess that means we can plan our trip to Hokkaido now that we've had our first anti-Covid jab," I joked, attempting to lighten the mood.

Though travel remained a distant dream, the idea brought a flicker of hope to our weary hearts.

Despite the physical and emotional toll, Bhanu worked tirelessly to maintain a sense of normalcy. He continued his academic work and consulting job, sprinkling our days with humor and pranks, political discussions, and engaging conversations about art, music, movies, and culture-- our shared passions.

Even amid his suffering, he continued doing things at home like a househusband, bringing home small surprises and ensuring that laughter never fully faded from our lives.

"Since you've been cooped up in the condo, I went shopping for you," he announced one day, holding up two pairs of underwear. "The lady cashier gave me a look like I'm a pervert," he added with a laugh.

"Yes, you are," I teased. "But thank you, my darling."

Our playful banter masked the harsh reality of his pain. He woke early not just for walks but to endure quiet moments of suffering, concealed from me to spare my heart.

"The teddy bear needed his early morning walks," he explained once, evading the truth with his usual humor. "Besides, he has to prepare his wife's breakfast."

Life continued, and for a time, Bhanu's health problems seemed under control, lulling me into believing that we would share the sunset of our lives together.

We cherished the small moments: the shared laughter, the comforting presence of his love, and the enduring strength of our bond.

Yet beneath the surface a silent battle raged, a relentless struggle against an invisible enemy, which -- like an ever-present sword of Damocles -- hung over us.

As the year 2022 started, the side effects of radiation therapy had not eased. On the contrary, it had gotten worse. There was more blood in his stool and rectal bleeding occurred more often.

He could not seem to find the right diet to prevent diarrhea and nausea from happening. Other times, constipation was his problem. Unable to eat many types of food, he lost a lot of weight.

"Let's go and check our house in Rangsit. I hope we can move there this year," I said in early June.

Bhanu looked at me with exhausted eyes. "I'm sorry, darling," he said. "I get tired very quickly these days. I can't drive anymore," he admitted with a twinge of sadness and resignation.

"That's okay, darling. We are actually in a good place in the condo. It is easy to order things here," I tried to lighten things.

Then I studied Bhanu's face. For the first time, I could sense his frustration that his health problems seemed to have no end. There was a look of quiet suffering but defiant look in his eyes. He looked back at me, smiling wanly.

"I better continue with my research for the article I'm writing," he said, retreating to the familiar comfort of academic work.

Days later, he was having night sweats again. Alarmed, I urged him to have colonoscopy and endoscopy but they did not show anything new.

"My oncologist said that my fatigue was due to loss of blood and the night sweats were another side effect of radiation. Nothing serious," he reported.

But his weight loss continued. His face was now gaunt. His eyes were sunken and surrounded by dark circles.

Still, Bhanu kept his usual routine.

"What about a cheese omelet for breakfast for my little girl on this beautiful day," Bhanu would ask on a typical day.

"I'd love that," I would answer.

"Cheese omelet, it is," he would say with a smile.

"Hey, have you read the joke I sent you," he asked.

The joke was about William Shakespeare and a nurse during vaccination. It ended with the nurse saying, "Wait until the *Twelfth Night*," when Shakespeare asked about adverse effects.

I laughed, not just at the humor but at Bhanu's ability to find lightness in our darkening world.

By the time July arrived, our frequent lighthearted moments had become a rare commodity. Bhanu's health struggles persisted, but he continued diligently with his research and writing.

As days progressed, he was often exhausted and morose, and became uncharacteristically irritated easily. I watched him recede into himself at times, silently battling demons I could not see but whose presence I felt in every room of our home.

Amid this challenging backdrop, he received a piece of happy news in August. "Darling, I've been invited to attend the Asian Economic Panel (AEP) in Seoul in October," he announced excitedly.

Despite retiring from teaching, he was still valued by his colleagues, still invited to this tri-annual gathering of economists across Asia.

His connection with the AEP, dating back to its inaugural meeting in April 2001, had always been more than academic. It was a chance to reunite with friends and engage in discussions that he found stimulating.

The anticipation of meeting his friends, especially Corina (Maria Socorro Gochoco Bautista from the University of the Philippines), Yuki (Shigeyuki Abe, Kyoto University), and Chandra (Prema-Chandra Athukorala, Australian National University), seemed to temporarily erase his daily struggles.

With Bhanu heading to Seoul, I decided it was a perfect chance to visit my family in Manila, something I had not done for three years. The sword of Damocles still hung above us. But, for a brief precious moment, we ignored it and carried on as if everything was okay.

The trip to Seoul appeared to breathe new life into Bhanu. He looked invigorated, cheerful, and brimming with plans when he met me at the airport on my return from Manila.

On our way home, Bhanu talked animatedly about the Seoul conference, the lively discussions and enjoyable dinners, and how Corina gifted us with *hopia*, a Filipino snack.

"That's great! I wasn't able to buy anything from Manila because of the typhoon," I replied happily.

"There's more good news," he said smiling. "I was invited to attend a conference in Tokyo in March. We are going."

I felt a rush of excitement. "Fantastic! We can stay a bit longer to look at the cherry blossoms," I said, already imagining the gardens in Tokyo that we would visit in early spring.

"Maybe we can travel north to Hokkaido," Bhanu replied, squeezing my hand. "And we must go back to Hakone and stay at Odakyu da Yama even if just for a day," he added excitedly.

The mention of Hakone brought back a flood of memories.

Hakone and Cherry Blossoms

The year 2019 was described by many newspapers as the best in human history (up to a point).

For us, it was a year of celebration - our fortieth anniversary, Bhanu's retirement, and a long-dreamed trip to enchanting Hakone, where thick bands of pinkish-white cherry blossoms floated in the hills like low-hanging clouds. I had always wanted to see cherry blossoms again since I first saw them in the spring of 1984 in Washington, DC.

It was our final year in the US, my graduation was forthcoming in May, and Bhanu was wrapping up his dissertation. A visit to Washington, DC during the peak of the cherry blossom festival served as a fitting farewell to the place where we had spent many exciting and memorable days.

It was a cold, overcast day in early April when we arrived in the US capital, but the biting chill quickly gave way to a breathtaking sight. Massive pink and white cherry blossoms were everywhere, transforming the Tidal Basin, the Washington Monument and beyond into an enchanting place of white and pink.

Fast forward to our visit to Japan in April 2019. While Tokyo's cherry blossoms had bid their farewell by late April, Hakone, nestled in higher elevations, presented an entirely different scene.

There, cherry trees heavy with blooms dotted the hills. They offered a spectacular display of nature's vibrant artistry that echoed the timeless allure of Washington, DC's cherry blossoms.

Hakone was a place untouched by time. The Odakyu da Yama Hotel where we stayed was perched on a hill overlooking Lake Ashi. The hotel's stately villa, built on a hill in 1911, exuded the quiet elegance of its era alongside modern comforts.

From our room, we gazed at the breathtaking view of the lake, with the enigmatic Mount Fuji looming majestically in the background. By day, the lake shimmered under the sunlight, its crystal-clear blue waters hosting tourist cruise boats. As night fell, tiny lights from fishing boats scattered across the darkened lake.

As soon as we settled in our room, we excitedly climbed the stairs to the hotel's tower, hoping to catch a view of the elusive mountain. But Fuji, in its mysterious way, hid behind thick clouds.

Disappointed, we retreated to an early dinner at the veranda. And there, as if teasing us, the mountain revealed itself, its snow-capped peak standing aloof, yet breathtaking in its grandeur.

During our stay, we strolled through the hotel's expansive garden. Boasting 3,000 azaleas of 70 varieties, they would have been enchanting in full bloom. Unfortunately, our visit was too early for the azaleas.

We decided to return in early May the following year.

As planned, our immediate focus was again on enjoying the cherry blossoms. After a wrong turn, our eventful bus ride eventually brought us to the Miyagawa River.

The quest for the entrance to its banks proved challenging until a kind old woman guided us to a nondescript wooden gate. Beyond the gate was a narrow footpath, flanked by blooming red and dark pink peonies.

The path led us to the riverbank.

A mesmerizing sight greeted us there -- a miles-long stretch of cherry trees, their branches heavy with dense light pink blossoms. When the wind blew, a gentle shower of delicate petals cascaded around us, a mesmerizing spectacle before settling on the ground and creating a delicate carpet.

Nature, it seemed, orchestrated this moment of beauty and serenity, with the only audible sounds being the murmur of water flowing gently in the river below.

On that spring day, the sky above painted itself in a clear, light blue hue, while a soft, cold breeze added a touch of magic to the atmosphere.

"I could stay here forever," Bhanu remarked, relishing the moment. "But we have to go to The Little Prince Museum before it closes."

And so, reluctantly we left the magical place of cherry blossoms. At the same time, we were eager to visit the Little Prince Museum, to pay homage to a literary figure who meant so much to both of us.

No book shaped our love story more than *The Little Prince*, by Antoine de Saint-Exupery.

An Evening by the Lake and *The Little Prince*

Bhanu and I first met at the International Rice Research Institute (IRRI) in Los Banos, Laguna, a misty, evergreen town at the foot of the legendary Mount Makiling in the Philippines. I was a 21-year-old research aide; he was 24, a newly-hired Economics lecturer at Thammasat University in Thailand.

During the two-week training, we barely exchanged words. Then, one late afternoon as I was leaving the office, Bhanu came to see me.

Wearing his favorite light blue, long-sleeved cotton shirt and black polyester pants, he stood out from the rest of the men who were wearing mainly denim jeans, or khaki pants and T-shirts, IRRI being an agricultural research institute where technical employees and scholars go out to the rice fields most of the time.

"Fancy having dinner with me this evening?" he asked, his voice unsteady and stammering slightly, his smiling eyes looking straight into mine.

I felt my face grow warm, aware that my colleagues were watching us, giggling.

Deep inside, my heart was jumping with joy. I had been waiting and hoping for days that Bhanu would ask me out. I wanted to play it cool. But, "Yes!" I replied, perhaps too eagerly.

That evening, Bhanu took me to a lakeside restaurant I had never been before. It was surrounded by bougainvilleas, its open capiz shell windows letting in the gentle evening breeze.

From the veranda, we watched the sunset over Laguna de Bay, the water reflecting hues of gold, orange and violet.

As we waited for our meal, I gazed up at the evening sky, now dotted with stars. "Look at the stars," I said smiling. "For you, my star will just be one of the many. That way, you will love watching all of them." I was trying to impress him.

"That's beautiful! You sound like a poet!" Bhanu said, eyes widening.

"Oh, I'm just quoting my favorite line from *The Little Prince*," I confessed.

"Do you know the book?" I asked.

"I'm afraid not," he replied.

"You should read it. It's a beautiful story. I've loved it since I was 17," I said.

Then I continued talking about the book, my words tumbling out. Bhanu listened, silent but attentive, his eyes reflecting the flickering candlelight.

As days passed, we grew closer discovering in each other a kindred spirit. It was like finding the other half of ourselves we did not know existed.

By the time his workshop ended and he had to return to Bangkok, we had already promised to spend our lives together-- a promise that would span the next 44 years.

On his last day in Los Banos, seeing my sadness mirroring his feelings, he took my hand and said, "Don't ever doubt my sincerity and faithfulness to you. Trust your heart." Then to my surprise, he added word for word:

"Now here is my secret, very simply: you can only see things clearly with your heart. What is essential is invisible to the eye."

Bhanu continued, "As the fox in *The Little Prince* said: 'You become responsible forever for what you have tamed.' I am now responsible for you for the rest of my life."

And he was.

Now in the taxi, the memory of that night lingered in my mind. Bhanu, sitting beside me, gave my hand a gentle squeeze. "What are you thinking? You are smiling," he said, his eyes gleaming.

I turned to him, meeting his familiar gaze. "Hakone," I replied. "What an enchanting place."

"We'll be back there in about five months," Bhanu said, his voice brimming with hope and anticipation.

Outside, the city stretched before us, the sun casting golden light over familiar streets.

Bhanu looked healthy and happy. He had just completed an economic article recently published online, and was already outlining a new book.

The world was emerging from two years of lockdowns and uncertainties. Thus, 2023 looked full of promises.

We rode home that day, unaware that the darkest days of our lives were already waiting just beyond the horizon.

One month later, Bhanu was diagnosed with terminal pancreatic cancer. In an instant, our world was turned upside down. Instead of continuing on his new book -- a project that brought him so much hope and purpose -- he was admitted to the hospital for more tests and initial treatment.

The Descent Begins

After spending a week in the hospital, Bhanu returned home, worn but relieved to be back.

He greeted me with a warm hug, the kind that would usually brighten my day, but this time I was alarmed as I felt the sharp edges of his frailty.

He did not speak of the daunting future that lay ahead for us, but his body betrayed him -- his once salt-and-pepper hair had turned stark white, his face was gaunt, and his smile, though present, felt like a mask.

His eyes, tinged with sadness, still held that stubborn determination, as if sheer willpower could keep him here with me.

"I'm fine," he said softly, catching the look on my face. His words tried to reassure me, but his voice was thinner, quieter, and less convincing than I wanted it to be.

I could tell how exhausted he was, as he wearily lay down on the bed. I joined him, curling into the crook of his arm, trying to give him strength.

As we held each other, the warmth of his body gave me a sense of hope that everything would be alright. I held onto him tightly, refusing to let go.

"He'll get better," I told myself. "He has to!"

Sensing my distress, he got up to assuage my feelings. Like his shadow, I followed him. And as usual, I clung to his strength, because it was easier than facing the truth.

Attempting to divert my attention from his perilous condition, he lightly recounted his days in the hospital, sounding as if nothing serious happened.

Instead of talking about himself and his illness, he cheerfully (or pretended to sound cheerful) recounted the visit of his good friend, Dr. Naris Chaiyasoot, and his wife, a doctor at the hospital.

So that I won't feel sorry about him, he told me about the other patient with terminal cancer in his ward, a man in his 30s with a young family.

He shared details of his adjusted diet--he could consume anything except fatty foods--and the supplementary nutrition essential to regain his lost weight and strength in preparation for the impending chemotherapy at the end of month.

To assure me that he was getting the necessary treatment, he showed me an array of medication to alleviate the numerous health problems plaguing him: persistent nausea, the ever-present mucus in his throat and lungs, and irregular bowel movements.

But it was the morphine that shook me.

I stared at the bottle in silence, my chest tightening. Morphine. A word I had only encountered in the grim corners of my reading about cancer.

Wasn't this for end-stage patients? A tiny pin pricked my heart as I held the bottle in my hand. This is it. It's real.

"Is he at that stage now?" I wondered, panic rising in my chest. But he sounded so optimistic just a few days ago....

I grappled with accepting the harsh reality. I still could not believe that Bhanu was gravely ill. He could not be.

I looked at him. His face was a picture of serenity. Although there was a trace of sadness in his eyes, they still twinkled when he looked at me.

"Does it hurt?" I whispered, holding his hand.

"Not all the time. Only the tenth rib hurts occasionally, but I can endure the pain," he replied, locking eyes with me, silently pleading for strength. He was doing his utmost to be resilient.

"I don't want you to suffer. Just take some," I managed to say, fighting back tears.

"I'm fine, don't worry. I'll go back to Siriraj in a week for genetic analysis and more tests to prepare for my chemo," he said stoically, assuring me.

Then, it was time to prepare dinner. I panicked. I did not know how to cook.

"Let's order food delivery," Bhanu suggested, well aware of my culinary shortcomings.

The first day after Bhanu's return passed without any incident.

That night, Bhanu slept alone in the sunroom. "The mucus keeps accumulating, and I don't want to disturb you," he said.

"But I want to hug my teddy bear," I protested, trying to coax him back.

"Teddy bear doesn't want to be hugged right now," he replied with a faint smile while gently caressing my arm. "His throat is clogged, and he's nauseous all the time."

I smiled back wanly. "Perhaps he did not want me to witness his pain," I thought, my heart breaking.

The next morning, Bhanu resumed his role as caregiver, as if nothing had changed. "Before anything else, I'll check your blood pressure," he said, concerned that it had not been monitored for a week. Despite his illness, he wanted to continue looking after me as he had always done.

During breakfast, he said quietly, "My doctor advised me to start putting everything in order."

He took those words to heart, spending the day meticulously packing his belongings -- piles of papers, diaries, notes, CDs, USBs, and an array of keepsakes from over four decades of teaching.

The sheer volume was overwhelming, a lifetime condensed into boxes. The weight of it mirrored the fleeting nature of time.

Even when he was in pain, he did not show it. Immersed in his task, he quietly sorted his belongings, occasionally retreating to the bathroom to clear the mucus from his throat.

He barely ate, managing only a few glasses of Ensure to sustain him. At dinner, he toyed with his food in silence, the day's efforts visibly draining him.

I tried to encourage him to eat, but at that moment, I realized how much had changed. Our roles had reversed. The man who had cared for me with such devotion now leaned on me.

A novice in caregiving, I was learning -- one dish, one laundered shirt, one small step at a time.

A Night of Lead in the Gloomy Sunroom

After dinner that night, Bhanu retired early to his room. Probably, he was drained from the heartbreaking task of assembling, arranging, and classifying his life's work - deciding what to keep and what to discard.

Whatever emotions he felt, he kept them tightly guarded. The awareness of his limited time on this earth must have gnawed at his heart and tormented his soul.

As I prepared to go to bed, I heard Bhanu going to the bathroom and returning to his room. Concerned, I called out across the hall, "Are you okay?"

"I'm fine," came his reply, followed by an eerie and melancholic silence.

Deciding not to disturb him, I lay down to sleep. However, a persistent uneasy feeling prompted me to check on Bhanu.

I crept toward his room, the stillness heightening my anxiety. Suddenly, Bhanu's moans shattered the silence, sending shivers through me.

In an instant, I was at his bedside. He was shivering, his teeth chattering, desperately attempting to cover himself with a thin blanket.

"I'm cold, cold, cold," he whispered.

I touched his forehead and jerked back. It was searingly hot. "Oh, my God! You're burning!"

My heart pounded like a hammer against stone, with adrenaline surging through me as if trying to break through my body's limitations.

My legs, unbound by the weight of my hemiplegia, seemed to find wings of their own, carrying me in defiance of my reality.

Frantically, I scoured the dressing table for an analgesic.

"Take this," I handed him a 500-mg paracetamol.

Briefly, the medicine seemed to stabilize his fever and trembling. But after a while, his temperature rose again.

"I'm cold, very cold. Socks! I need socks," he pleaded, his voice quivering.

Swiftly, I darted into our bedroom, hands trembling, rummaging through Bhanu's cabinet drawers for his socks. Clutching them, an extra blanket, and a face towel, I rushed back to his side.

Delirious with fever, he thrashed and resisted as I struggled to put the socks on.

"Please, please let me put on your socks!" I pleaded, grappling to hold his violently shaking feet.

Struggling against his flailing, I finally succeeded in dressing him, wrapping him in an extra layer of warmth. He was lost in a world of pain. Blankets tumbled, chaos ensued, but with persistence, I was able to cover him once more.

By now, Bhanu was in extreme agony. He was turning his head left and right, his eyes rolling.

"Cold! Cold! Cold!" He kept muttering, lost in torment.

Hoping to get some help, I called his elder brother. It was close to midnight. After several rings, he answered.

"It is very late. Call your son," he said with exasperation. Then he hung up.

Our son lives with his wife and newborn daughter about 45 kilometers from our condo. I called him, no answer. I left a message.

I called the condo manager. No answer.

Feeling abandoned with nobody to help us, I cradled Bhanu in my tiny arms, my body aching but unwilling to let go. I glanced out the bedroom window.

Midnight cloaked the world in silence, save for the faint hum of vehicles on the street below. The lights of the buildings blinked in the distance, cold and unfeeling, as if mocking my helplessness.

Then his eyes began to flutter shut. Panic seized me, and I clutched him tighter. "Stay with me!" I cried, my voice breaking. "Don't go! I can't let you go now, not ever!"

Desperate, I called an ambulance, my trembling fingers fumbling with the phone. "We'll be there in ten minutes," replied the driver.

Those minutes felt like a lifetime as I watched his fragile chest rise and fall, willing it to continue. Time seemed to stretch endlessly, every second filled with the terror of losing him.

When the ambulance and emergency team arrived, a wave of relief washed over me, momentarily soothing the panic that had gripped me.

But what came next was unexpected. I felt a strange strength surge through me, as if some hidden reservoir had been tapped.

Suddenly, I was not the helpless wife cradling her ailing husband -- I was methodical, mechanical, and detached, moving with precision as I relayed his condition to the paramedics.

It was as though I had become one of them, a part of their team. There was no room for tears or trembling hands now; only action mattered.

Looking back, I realize it must have been a release of adrenaline -- a coping mechanism after the storm of emotion that had engulfed me just minutes before. In those moments, I was not panicking; I was focused, almost numb.

But beneath the surface, a quiet fear lingered, waiting to rise again when the task at hand was over.

As we rushed to the emergency room, a long night began, a relentless cycle set to repeat for the next five months.

It was already past midnight, yet life's drama continued in the emergency room -- patients in need, an injured boy, an elderly woman, and a young man. Amidst it all, a sympathetic nurse offered me a chair, a place to sit and to hold Bhanu's hand, to reassure him and myself.

After a tense half an hour later, the emergency room doctor talked to me.

"Your husband has a bacterial infection. We still need more tests to find out the cause. He has to be admitted," he said gently.

Behind him was the admission officer. She said that the only available room was a royal suite at 40,000 baht (approximately US$1,100) per night, a staggering cost. She then asked me if I would take it.

In the early hours, exhausted and frustrated, I snapped at the absurdity of her question.

"Okay, Madam, please sign this admission form," she said, her sympathy a small comfort in the chaos. Everyone in the emergency room, in their own way, shared in our struggle.

The night pressed on, and as Bhanu was prepared to move to his room, he was still required to have an abdominal ultrasound.

At last, my son arrived, having rushed to the hospital after reading my frantic message. His presence brought a small measure of comfort, though the night's ordeal was far from over.

Silently, we accompanied Bhanu, walking together along the darkened, deserted corridors from the emergency room to the radiology department for an ultrasound.

Nearly an hour later, my husband, frail yet resilient, was wheeled to the opulence of his hospital suite. By now, a somber December dawn was breaking, heralding the arrival of a time that would test our strength in the coming days and months.

Although there was a large extra bedroom in Bhanu's hospital suite, I slept on the sofa bed next to him to make sure that I was around just in case he needed something during the remaining hours of the long night.

The test results came the next day. Bhanu's fever was the result of bacterial growth on the metal stent.

Two days later, after receiving a steady dose of antibiotics, the infection was mostly under control and Bhanu's body temperature was back to normal.

Later, he felt so much better that he even took my photo clowning to cheer him up.

That would be the last time he used his phone's camera.

On the eve of Bhanu's discharge, Dr. Kulpatra Sirodom (Ajarn Nui), a dear friend, and Ms. Arpa, our condominium manager, paid a brief visit carrying a basket of fruits.

Despite everyone's attempt to project an air of positivity, an undercurrent of unspoken fears lingered. As I escorted them to the door later, Ajarn Nui embraced me, gently planting kisses on my cheeks as her tears finally fell.

For the first time, in that poignant moment, I felt the looming presence of mortality. Looking at my husband resting on his bed and appearing much better than two nights earlier, I fought back my tears, remembering how close we were to losing him.

"Dr. Charlie said I will probably be able to go home tomorrow if the fever does not return. Then you can have a good rest," he said cheerfully.

"He recommended that I eat only cooked food. And everything must be clean to prevent any infection."

"That means I will have to cook your food. I do not trust these food deliveries," I said.

"I do not want you to get very tired cooking my food and doing everything else. Let us hope I get stronger soon so I can help you," he said, sounding hopeful.

Unable to trust my voice, fearing it might betray my emotions, I turned away, my gaze landing on the basket of fruits. A vibrant California orange seemed to beam at me.

"Don't you just love that orange?" I said changing the subject, pretending to be happy. I did not realize I could be an excellent actress, acting as if everything was all right, that the world held no cause for worry.

"Yes," Bhanu replied. "It looks like the orange I gave you at IRRI."

"That was almost 45 years ago," I answered softly, my mind drifting to that pivotal day when Bhanu took the courage to talk to me and offered an orange, initiating our forty-four years of shared existence.

"Yes, I remember that afternoon very well. Your face was as red as a ripe tomato," he said smiling.

My heart was heavy as my mind was filled with memories of that time when our lives were young, and our journey together had just begun.

Here and now, in the confines of the hospital room, quiet questions echoed within me: "How long do we have? How long does he have?"

The weight of those questions was suffocating, yet I pushed them aside, clinging to hope, clinging to him. I could not bear to let fear rob us of the present moment.

Before the shadows of my thoughts could deepen, the doctor came in to check Bhanu's progress.

The next day, he was fit enough to go home.

"From now on, you will sleep in our bed, beside me," I told Bhanu when we got home.

"But you might get disturbed when I have to get up at night," he pointed out.

"That's fine. I'll be monitoring your temperature regularly, and I can't bear the thought of another emergency in the dead of the night," I explained.

"Sure thing, Mommy. I promise not to let it happen again," he reassured playfully.

Later, as the weeks turned to months, the sunroom -- once a space of light and laughter -- grew darker, mirroring Bhanu's declining condition.

Our world was shrinking, and every moment together carried the weight of what we knew, but refused to believe, was coming.

Goodbye, Thammasat

Just two days into his recovery, Bhanu, with his indomitable spirit, returned to Thammasat University (TU), his cherished alma mater and the institution where he had imparted knowledge for more than four enriching decades.

Perhaps his recent brush with death had made him realize the urgency of clearing his office, meeting his former assistants and colleagues, and bidding them a heartfelt farewell. It was a poignant act, turning the final page in the book of his academic journey as he faced the reality of his terminal illness.

Thammasat held a profoundly special place in Bhanu's life. As his alma mater - Latin for "nourishing mother" -- it was where his youthful intellect was nurtured. Here, in the fertile grounds of academia, his idealistic worldview took shape, and his simple yet profound life goals crystallized: an insatiable quest for knowledge and an unwavering commitment to the art of teaching.

He arrived at TU as a 17-year-old freshman in 1971. Except for a year pursuing a master's degree at the London School of Economics and five years of doctoral studies at Johns Hopkins University in Baltimore, he spent his entire adult life within the challenging world of TU.

Over the course of an illustrious 41-year teaching career, he ascended to the roles of vice-rector and dean of the Faculty of Economics. Along the way, he authored numerous articles, books, and publications.

Yet, among his many accomplishments, he treasured most the legacy of the hundreds of students he mentored -- many of whom went on to achieve remarkable success in their lives.

In his crowded office, Bhanu and his assistants undertook the arduous task of sifting through papers, books, and mementos. Together, they decided which ones to discard, to keep, or to donate to the library.

In the end, among the myriad items in his room, he chose to take home only one thing -- an old, leather briefcase, a precious gift from his late mother 46 years ago when he left for England. He brought it home as a reminder of his mother's love and devotion, and as a source of strength to carry him through the time he had left.

That weathered briefcase was more than just an object of utility; it encapsulated the enduring affection of Bhanu's mother and the deep bonds of his family.

As the youngest child, he had been cherished -- the pride and joy of his family, who celebrated his achievements with unwavering support. Even as a young boy, he had garnered recognition, winning a painting award from none other than His Majesty King Bhumibol Adulyadej of Thailand.

His academic journey mirrored those early successes. Graduating with a BA in Economics from TU in just three and a half years, he earned First Class honors, securing a prestigious Thai government scholarship for a master's degree at the esteemed London School of Economics.

Amidst the challenges of studying in a foreign land, his elder sister Nayana (Yui) became his steadfast pillar of support. Their bond was more than just familial; he idolized her, seeing in her great beauty and wisdom, while she, in turn, saw in him the little brother who needed nurturing.

During his student days in London, Yui graciously opened her flat to him, providing him with the comfort and stability needed to navigate the rigors of his studies. Their time together in London became a treasured chapter in their sibling relationship.

After enduring emotionally draining hours with his assistants in the office, Bhanu faced one more crucial task -- ensuring my well-being when he was no longer around.

"I have just instructed my bank that you are the sole beneficiary of all my accounts," he texted me that afternoon. His words blinked ominously on my screen, a stark reminder of his mortality. I felt as if a dagger had pierced my heart.

Despite the gravity of the moment, Bhanu attempted to lift both my spirits and his own. "You are a rich woman now," he playfully quipped. "You could open your own bake shop."

"And you just became as poor as a church mouse," I replied, forcing a joking tone to mask the heaviness in my heart.

But beneath our light-hearted banter, the unspoken sorrow lingered. As I had so often done before, I went into denial. How could he be so ill when he was still so full of life and humor?

"I have to stay at Siriraj today until tomorrow," he said. "They want to check my genetic makeup. I hope you will be all right alone again."

"Don't worry, I'll be fine," I reassured him. "I'm going to bake a fruitcake for Christmas. I hope it turns out all right. It's my first time to do so."

"And I would be your poor guinea pig," he replied, his words carrying a touch of playful affection.

His humor was his shield, his way of facing the inevitable. And for a fleeting moment, I let myself believe in the illusion that everything would be alright.

Between our exchanges, the harsh reality of his illness loomed, ever-present yet unspoken.

Christmas: A Time of Sadness

Christmas is no longer the joyous season I knew. I stopped listening to the Christmas carols that I loved. When the holiday season came, all I wanted was to hibernate somewhere, in a cave, under the ground, any place where I could hide away from all the memories of what Christmas used to be.

Since our marriage in 1979, Christmas held a special place in our hearts. We always adorned a Christmas tree and embraced the Filipino tradition of *noche buena* on Christmas Eve, a hearty midnight dinner enjoyed after returning from Christmas Eve Mass.

Despite being a non-practicing Buddhist, Bhanu enthusiastically joined in my Catholic Christmas celebration, to make me happy.

"Let's put up the Christmas tree when I get stronger," he suggested the following morning after he returned from Siriraj.

"That would be fantastic!" I replied, feigning delight while holding back tears.

"This year, let's give our friends copies of your book instead of the usual fruitcake," Bhanu suggested with a beaming smile, his pride in me evident. "By the way, your fruitcake looks fantastic. I hope it tastes as good as it looks."

For the first time in days, his words made me happy. His pride in my modest achievements momentarily lifted my heavy heart.

"I hope the books arrive before Christmas," I replied with anticipation. "And let's enjoy the fruitcake on Christmas Eve; it will have aged perfectly by then."

By mid-December, the tree remained unadorned. The silk poinsettias, once vibrant with festive spirit, sat untouched on the table, gathering dust.

As Christmas Day approached, Bhanu's struggle worsened. He was always nauseous and the cancer pain was more frequent. Still, he resisted morphine.

"I hate taking morphine -- it gives me hallucinations. I can't sleep," he complained, dark circles shadowing his sunken eyes.

Mucus clogged his throat, making each breath a battle. The doctors offered no real remedy. Eating became nearly impossible -- every bite was a struggle against nausea.

On Christmas Eve, the special dishes I had painstakingly prepared, including the perfectly baked fruitcake, remained untouched. I did not attend Christmas Eve Mass; I could not leave his side.

Gloom greeted us on Christmas Day. After a fitful night's sleep, Bhanu rose early to prepare for his trip to his brother's house that afternoon where he would spend the night before his appointment with the oncologist the following morning.

As part of his morning ritual -- a ritual that had become almost second nature to him for the last seventeen years, he measured my blood pressure. "I'm worried about you. Your blood pressure has been above normal lately," he said softly while stroking my arm.

"I wish I didn't have to go to the hospital so I could take care of you." He held my gaze a moment longer than usual, wistfully.

That would be the last time.

Later that morning, a couple of workers arrived to remove furniture and potted plants from the laundry area. We planned to convert it into Bhanu's lounging room, where he could enjoy the sunlight early in the morning.

When Bhanu saw the workers preparing to dispose of our artificial Christmas tree, he looked at me with pleading eyes. "Are we throwing that away too?" he asked, trying to suppress the quiver in his voice.

"Yes," I replied, swallowing hard while gazing at his sad face. "We need the space. We'll buy a new one next Christmas."

Bhanu's eyes followed the tree as it was carried away. It was so old that its upper branch had broken, which Bhanu had fixed with a long red ribbon. As the tree passed him, the tail of the ribbon brushed his shoulder, as if to kiss him goodbye.

When it was time for him to leave, he gave me a brief hug, his arms lighter, almost weightless around me. A month after his diagnosis, Bhanu has grown thinner, frailer. His khaki shirt fluttered around him like a sail. His pants sagged, the tightened belt keeping them from falling. Even his strides were now much slower.

At the door, I instinctively moved to follow him but stopped, sensing the weight he carried. He turned to look at me one last time, his eyes glistened with unspoken sorrow and apology.

He knew how much I loved spending Christmas with him. For over forty years, we had spent this day together--feasting, watching reruns of Christmas movies, letting ourselves be carefree, even for just a day.

But this year, there were no carols playing. The festive food sat cold and untouched in the refrigerator. And the specter of his illness loomed over us like a dark shroud.

When the door finally closed behind him, the floodgates broke. I collapsed into tears.

"Are you okay? I'm worried about you," he texted that night from his brother's house. Texting offered a refuge. It shielded us from seeing the pain on each other's faces.

"I'm alright," (no, I wasn't) I replied, expressing more with stickers than words could convey.

"My back hurts!" he texted back.

"Because of cancer? Take some morphine," I suggested, concerned.

"No! You just jumped on my back," his usual joke, lightening the mood.

"Sleep tight, don't let the bed bug bite," I said.

"Sweet dreams," he replied, "I'll see you tomorrow," a digital embrace followed our virtual conversation.

The next day, he arrived at Siriraj before 8 a.m. His scheduled appointment passed. One hour. Then two. Then three.

By the eighth hour, his oncologist finally saw him -- no chemotherapy, just another discussion about preparing for treatment and suggestions to gain weight.

"Eight hours? How could they treat you like that?" I fumed. "Don't they know you're very sick?"

"There were others like me," he said, ever patiently.

"Your son just berated everyone at the hospital," he added, sighing.

Exhausted, Bhanu slept early that night. The next day, feeling more rested, he was in good spirits.

"Darling, I think you're getting paranoid," he teased. "This must be the sixth time you've checked my temperature today."

"I'm really worried about you after spending almost eight hours in that hospital and being exposed to so many sick people and potential infections," I confessed while preparing his Ensure drink.

"It's 36 degrees," I reported.

"See, I am fine. I don't feel anything except for some pain in my tenth rib," he said, smiling bravely.

"Why don't you take morphine?" I asked.

"That's okay. I can bear it. It is not that painful," he sounded confident and strong.

Around five o'clock in the afternoon, I checked his temperature again. "It's 36.5 degrees," I said, alarmed.

"That's still normal and I feel good," Bhanu said reassuringly.

That evening, I pleaded with him to eat.

"If you finish this soup and five spoonsful of mashed potatoes, you'll make me the happiest wife alive."

"Yes, Mommy," he said playfully, but struggling through the meal.

He barely finished half. When I scolded him, he promised to drink Ensure before bed. It was a promise he would not keep.

A Harrowing Encore

After dinner, Bhanu took a shower, moving slowly, deliberately. If he felt any pain, he did not say a word -- he saw how busy I was with the dishes. The last thing he wanted was to be a burden.

Earlier, I had noticed his temperature rising. Worried, I checked it again once he was in bed. The numbers glared back at me -- 37 degrees. Higher than before dinner. An ominous sign of a harrowing encore.

"As a precaution, take an analgesic," I urged gently, though anxiety was already tightening its grip on me.

"You're the boss," he agreed weakly.

I returned to the kitchen, scrubbing dishes in a futile attempt to distract myself from the dread gnawing at my chest.

Thirty minutes later, I checked again. 38 degrees.

My heart skipped a beat. God. Not again.

"Darling, your temperature is rising, and the analgesic isn't working," I said, my voice barely steady. Bhanu lay silent, suffering, his eyes half-closed.

"I'll call an ambulance," I said with my teeth chattering. He did not protest.

While waiting, instinct told me to place a plastic sheet beneath him. His once-strong body lay inert, his stomach churning.

"Darling, turn to your right, please!" I pleaded, my own body straining under his weight. With a final heave, I slid the sheet into place just in time.

"Darling, I have to go to the toilet," he gasped desperately.

I rushed to him, but I was too late.

"It's alright," I whispered, forcing a reassuring smile. "I'll help you change."

His face burned with embarrassment as he apologized again and again.

"Don't worry about it," I consoled him, wiping away both the mess and the tears I refused to shed. Seeing him like this -- so vulnerable, so unlike the strong man I had always known -- shattered me. I wish I could shield him from this storm.

At last, the emergency team arrived. It was nearly 9 p.m. Just like before, the doctor ran a series of tests. Just like before, the results echoed the same refrain -- bacterial infection.

Bhanu had to be admitted again. A cruel encore, just two weeks after the last.

It was December 27. Four days before the dawn of an uncertain new year.

The next morning, I leaned over his bed. "I have to go home to shower," I told him. "The hospital shower is too slippery and it has only one handrail."

"Alright," Bhanu replied barely able to speak. "But come back soon. I don't like it when you're not here."

The infection still raged inside him despite the antibiotic drip coursing through his veins.

After shower, my phone rang. It was the hospital.

My heart nearly stopped.

"We're transferring your husband to ICU," the nurse said calmly.

Panic clawed at my throat. "Why?"

"There was a lot of blood in his stool this morning. He was in pain."

I wanted to cry, but I steeled myself.

"The doctors recommend a colonoscopy and endoscopy tomorrow," she continued. "Only liquid food and strong laxatives today."

Good Lord. He's already skin and bones. This is the last thing he needs.

When the call ended, my phone buzzed again. This time, it was a text from Bhanu.

"Good news! You don't have to return today. Since I'll be in ICU, you can sleep well tonight."

Then, as if softening the blow: "But I will miss you."

"I'll miss my teddy bear, too," I replied, my eyes watering.

Later that afternoon, another message.

"There's nothing wrong with my colon. Just the same radiation side effect that's been bugging me for over a year."

Then: "Where have you been? I don't like it when I don't hear from you."

"Sorry! I went out for a haircut. Here's a photo."

"Gorgeous!"

"Liar."

"Hope to see you soon."

"Will you be back in your room today?" I asked, relieved that he seemed to be feeling better.

"The doctor says I'll move out of ICU tomorrow if my fever goes down."

Another night alone. For both of us.

On New Year's Eve, Bhanu was transferred to a regular room, though the fever still lingered.

"Hey, what are you up to?" I asked when I entered, relieved to see him smiling.

In front of him was a tri-ball incentive spirometer -- a small device with three chambers, each containing a ball.

"I'm supposed to blow hard enough to lift all three balls at the same time," he explained.

"Did you?" I asked, happy to see him engaged in something.

"Only two." He chuckled. "I've been in bed too long. My lungs need a workout."

He spent much of the day practicing, determined to succeed.

Bhanu said goodbye to a year of trials and tribulations, welcoming an uncertain new year within the sterile walls of his hospital room.

In the past, we would have been gleefully stuffing our mouths with 12 grapes at midnight and drinking champagne. Now, we sat in a dimly lit hospital room, surrounded by the smell of antiseptic and medications.

While the world outside erupted in celebration, I sat watching my husband sleep fitfully, his arm hooked to an antibiotic drip, his body exhausted from battle.

Inside his room, we could not hear the fireworks.

Instead, the only sound was the anguished cries of a man in another room, calling for his mother.

Five days after his admission, the infection refused to loosen its grip.

His body had become a battleground of medications - antibiotics, anti-allergy drugs, potassium infusions, blood clot preventatives, saline solutions. Morphine. Pethidine. Paracetamol. Suppositories. Anesthetics from the colonoscopy.

"Medications. And more medications!" Bhanu groaned one day, eyeing the rows of multi-colored pills lined up before him.

Some before meals. Some after. Some before sleep. And some in the middle of the night, like morphine, when the pain from cancer attacked.

Or as Bhanu called it, the bad guy.

Chapter Two
January: A Promise of Hope

"Hope is the thing with feathers-
That perches in the soul -
And sings the tune without the words -
And never stops - at all."
- Emily Dickinson, "Hope is the Thing with Feathers"

With a 24-hour antibiotic drip flooding his veins, Bhanu fought off the lingering bacterial infection, even as he struggled to inflate the spirometer to keep his lungs strong.

Fever-free for a week, and with lab results confirming the infection was under control, his doctors finally deemed him fit to go home.

Before we left the hospital, his doctor issued stark instructions: "Extreme hygiene is paramount. No fresh juices, everything sterilized, even his toothbrush."

With the bacterial infection subdued, at least for now, our focus shifted back to the frightening specter of Bhanu's pancreatic cancer. Without wasting time, we requested an urgent consultation with an oncologist.

Before the consultation, Bhanu underwent another blood test. The oncologist, his kindly face lined with years of experience in countless battles, studied the results and spoke gently.

"Chemotherapy needs to start immediately," he advised. "Your CA levels have doubled in a month - 180,000 U/ml. Time is of the essence."

For a moment, the room fell silent as Bhanu and I absorbed the latest numbers. I shivered, remembering the initial count -- already impossibly high. Now, it was far worse.

My heart pounded as I stole a glance at Bhanu. He remained quiet, staring at his hands. Then, he looked up, searching my eyes, and said with firm resolve, "Darling, I would like to have chemotherapy in this hospital."

With only Bhanu's well-being in mind, I agreed without hesitation. It would be expensive, but after his harrowing experiences in two government hospitals, we both knew this was our best option. This hospital was renowned, drawing patients from all over the world, and it was less than a ten-minute drive from our condominium.

Still, questions crowded my mind. Knowing the devastating side effects of chemotherapy, I asked the oncologist about alternative treatments.

"If he doesn't have chemotherapy, the cancer will spread very quickly -- probably within three months," he explained. "With chemotherapy, hopefully we can slow it down."

"Probably, hopefully." I exhaled at the uncertainty of those words. Nobody truly knew for sure. But Bhanu had already started packing his things, determined to go home.

The question of chemotherapy was settled. The doctors would begin his treatment in two weeks. But before that, Bhanu had to be prepared -- with an entire arsenal of medications.

Each prescription was a reminder that this was not just cancer. It was a war being fought on many fronts.

By January, eating had become a full-blown quiet battle. Bhanu's appetite had nearly vanished, and what little he managed to eat often came back up – with nausea, vomiting, and sometimes painful bloating. At times, he battled constipation. For all these, the doctors gave him four different medications to help with digestion, reduce nausea and prevent vomiting. Another pill to prevent constipation. More pills to manage the side effects of the others.

Then there was the ever-present risk of infection. His immune system, already compromised, made him dangerously vulnerable. To guard against bacteria, the doctors prescribed three kinds of antibiotics. And, the list did not stop there.

To support his bones: Vitamin D

To protect his nerves: Vitamin B complex

To balance electrolytes: potassium

To raise dangerously low blood protein level: human albumin infusion

To loosen the mucus in his lungs and throat and to reduce the endless flow of saliva that refused to let him rest: more medication.

Bhanu had to take his medication before or after his meal. I would line the capsules and tablets in front of his plate like a battalion of soldiers preparing for war. Each would serve a purpose: to help him eat, to ease his discomfort, and to keep his body functioning just enough for the battles ahead.

Armed with this vast fortification, we finally left the hospital. After nearly two weeks, Bhanu's discharge brought both relief and trepidation. The doctor's warnings hung heavy in the air, a stark reminder of the fragile balance we now lived within.

"It sure is nice to be home," Bhanu murmured as we stepped inside our condominium.

The windows stood wide open, allowing the wind to flow freely. Sunlight streamed into our bedroom, a stark contrast to the sterile, air-conditioned confines of the hospital room.

It was a moment of solace, however fleeting, in a battle far from over.

But Bhanu's medication regimen was a constant reminder of the long fight ahead. Every morning and night, the kitchen table was filled with bottles and blister packs. I lined them up, trying to keep track -- as if by doing so, I could impose order on the silent chaos.

It was relentless and with each carefully measured dose, I was reminded how much Bhanu's body was enduring -- how much it was fighting just to survive the war raging inside him.

Chicken Soup and Soft-boiled Eggs

Even after three years, I still cannot bring myself to boil eggs without feeling a lump in my throat. The sight of them takes me back to those days when soft-boiled eggs and chicken soup were among the only foods Bhanu could eat.

Every day, my stomach churned as I sterilized utensils, plates, and glasses in a pan of boiling water. Steam rose in thick clouds, clinging to my face, blurring my vision.

No matter how careful I was, I imagined an invisible swarm of bacteria waiting to attack. Worse, with only one usable hand, things constantly slipped through my grasp like greased eels, sending me into an endless cycle of washing and rewashing.

Ensure -- the sweet-tasting supplement that had sustained Bhanu for months -- now had to be taken precisely two hours before or after his antibiotics or they would not work as effectively. That meant my entire day revolved around the clock, each task scheduled with precision.

But the hardest battle was not the sterilizing or the scheduling, it was getting Bhanu to eat enough.

He needed strength for chemotherapy, yet his appetite had all but disappeared. The nausea lingered despite the stent. Most days, he could only manage a few spoonsful of mashed potato and sips of chicken soup.

"I can eat a soft-boiled egg in the morning," he said one day.

"That's great!" I replied, seizing the small victory.

So, mornings became soft-boiled eggs and peeled apple slices. Lunch was chicken soup with bits of carrot or soft lumps of potato. Dinner? Chicken soup again.

"Aren't you tired of chicken soup?" I asked him one day. "How about I make risotto?"

Bhanu's eyes twinkled with amusement. "I love my wife's chicken soup," he said. "But I'll eat whatever she serves me, of course. Let's try your risotto."

It was a disaster. But he ate a few spoonful - more than his usual intake offering me his usual vote of confidence.

Although weak from eating so little, Bhanu still insisted on walking, pacing between our bedroom and the sunroom, a five-meter stretch.

"I've done ten rounds already," he would say, his voice proud despite his frailty. "Time for my Ensure. Then I'll do five more."

Walking had always been his way of staying strong. In Baltimore, forty years earlier, it was how we got around. During our first month there, we lived two miles from Homewood campus, where he attended classes. Every day, he walked the four-mile round trip, no matter the weather.

Tired as he was when he got home, he still helped with dinner because he knew I was a terrible cook, preferring to toss frozen meals into the oven.

"I'll cook *Kai Palo*," he would say, his way of telling me he missed Thai food. I would be delighted, both for the meal and the reprieve from cooking. That pattern continued for the next forty-four years.

One evening, he returned home with a boyish smile. "I've decided to take you for a walk at this fantastic place," he said, eyes bright with excitement. "But I won't tell you more. Just wait till Saturday."

That weekend, I hummed an old song as we set out on foot. After a mile, passing a path lined with gray mug wort and sun-bleached switchgrass, we arrived at an ornate, century-old gate. The wrought iron creaked softly as we pushed it open, and the air carried the scent of late-summer roses and lavender.

"This is Sherwood Gardens," Bhanu said, his voice bubbling with pride. "I pass by here every day. That's why I never get tired of walking."

Inside, stately 19th and early 20th-century homes stood shoulder to shoulder, their gardens bursting with the last gasps of summer color. Asters in lavender and deep purple swayed in the breeze, and goldenrods shimmered like miniature suns against trees just beginning their autumn transformation.

Birds flitted overhead, their calls filling the crisp air as they prepared for migration.

The fading flowers reminded me of aging women clinging to the remnants of youth and beauty, defying time.

For a couple of hours, we wandered through that hidden oasis, savoring the sights, the scents, the moment.

I smiled wistfully, remembering those carefree days before the battles began. When we were in the springtime of our lives, and the world still lay ahead unfolding with promise, as we walked step by step on quiet paths beneath a bright, cloudless sky.

Birthday

"Happy birthday, darling," I whispered, kissing him on the morning of his 69th birthday.

"Thank you, darling," he replied, his smile full of gratitude. We both knew how precious this milestone was. And yet, the cancer loomed like a shadow over the day, whispering the same unspoken question: How much time do we have left?

Bhanu never liked celebrating his birthday. He hated being reminded of his age.

This year was no different. We observed it quietly, just the two of us, eating soft-boiled rice and egg soup. I followed an internet recipe precisely, hoping to give him something comforting.

"Fantastic soup," he said, smiling as he set down the spoon.

I smiled back, but inside, I was praying. Praying that he would not have another medical emergency. Praying that the weight of it all -- the physical pain, the mental exhaustion, the constant apologies he offered for being a "burden" -- would not break him.

Praying for just a little more time.

Chemotherapy Port, January 22

On the surface our life was a surreal business as usual while we waited for his first chemotherapy.

Bhanu continued his daily "walks", listening to Buddhist chants on his CD player, chatting with friends online, and taking occasional rest. I spent my days doing housework, trying to improve my cooking, and not thinking of what lies ahead.

The almost peaceful rhythm of our daily life hid the seriousness of Bhanu's illness. We never discussed it. There were no talks about what I should do if he was no longer around. It was a topic that we both could not bring up.

Bhanu believed deeply, or wanted to believe, that the chemotherapy would work, and that he would be around for a few more years. It was the very thing I had been praying for.

As the day of the first chemotherapy approached, I was filled with anxiety, imagining the worst side effects

Bhanu would experience and how totally I was unprepared to handle this new challenge.

Two weeks after Bhanu was discharged, we found ourselves back in the hospital. This time, for the placement of a chemotherapy port in his chest.

Bhanu's oncologist explained the necessity of the procedure -- how chemotherapy, a brutal but necessary poison, would be delivered directly into his bloodstream through a device implanted under his skin.

As the doctor spoke, my mind wandered onto the word "port", imagining a harbor where ships docked and departed. But this was not a place of safe refuge, it was an entryway for the battle that lay ahead.

My heart pounded as I thought about the incision they would make in Bhanu's chest, the foreign object they would embed beneath his skin.

I glanced at him, searching for any sign of unease, but he was listening intently, nodding along, absorbing the information with quiet resolve. He always had an ability to stay composed in the face of bad news, but I knew the weight he carried.

The doctor continued, his voice clinical, methodical: "A chemotherapy port is a small disc or reservoir, made of plastic or metal, with a rubber seal at the top. A thin, soft, flexible catheter runs from the disc into a large vein. This allows for easier, less painful chemotherapy administration."

Less painful. The phrase lingered in the air like a cruel joke. Nothing about this was painless.

Bhanu exhaled slowly and said, "I'm ready to have the chemport." No hesitation, no trace of fear.

He had already made peace with the path ahead.

Getting better was all that mattered to him.

Before the procedure, the doctors ordered a CT scan to assess the spread of the cancer. I sat beside Bhanu as we waited for the results, my hands clenched together in my lap.

When the report came back, it read like a battlefield map, marking the territories the disease had already claimed:

The tumor had grown, reaching the left adrenal gland, curving near the stomach, the kidney, the spleen.

Metastasis in the peritoneum, the omentum, the umbilicus.

A lesion on his tenth rib, another place where the cancer had set up camp.

The words blurred before my eyes. We had known the cancer was spreading, but seeing it laid out so starkly made it harder to ignore the truth we had been trying to outrun.

Still, we clung to the plan -- the fourth chemotherapy session, scheduled for early March, would tell us if the treatment was working.

The morning of the chemport surgery, we left our condo before six in the morning. Neither of us had eaten. There was no room for hunger on days like this.

At the hospital, they prepped Bhanu for the procedure. Before they wheeled him away, he turned to me and smiled.

"It'll probably take a couple of hours," he said. "Go have a good breakfast."

His words, so casual, so him, hit me like a punch to the gut. Even now, facing yet another surgery, he was thinking of me.

I squeezed his hand, a silent response. Thank you for still caring for me, even when you are the one suffering.

He waved as the attendants wheeled him into the operating room. I forced a smile, but my throat tightened. I stood there, watching until he disappeared through the doors, willing myself not to cry.

A Moment of Normalcy

Bhanu spent the night in the hospital to recover. The next day, we returned home. He was already looking ahead, eager for his first chemotherapy session a week later. His body had been cut open, a foreign object placed inside him, yet he barely seemed to register the discomfort.

The cancer was relentless, but so was he.

A few days later, I had to go out for a couple of hours to meet a friend and sign my book. I hesitated to leave him alone, but Bhanu would not hear of it.

"I'm very proud of you," he said, beaming. "I wish I could drive you there myself."

"It's okay," I reassured him. "I won't be long."

I hovered near the door, reluctant to go. "Don't forget to drink your Ensure at three. I already put it in the fridge."

He gave me a playful look. "I'll be fine. Go. Have fun. Take photos!"

Even now, his first instinct was to take care of me.

As I stepped out, I realized how much these small, ordinary moments meant. A simple exchange about a meal, a farewell before a procedure, a lingering touch before he was wheeled away.

These were the fragile, precious threads holding our life together -- and I held onto them with all my strength.

First chemo, January 29

One week after the chemport was placed in his chest, Bhanu had his first chemotherapy session.

The day before, he carefully prepared his things -- clothes, mobile phone, a notepad, and the latest copy of *The Economist* - as if he was heading to an economics seminar rather than a hospital.

As we stepped out of the elevator, my heart skipped a beat. The words ONCOLOGY WARD loomed on the white, spotless walls, staring at us with malevolent eyes. I could almost hear the insidious voice of cancer whispering, "I got you; there's no escaping me this time".

The ward was eerily silent, as if any noise might disrupt the fragile battle taking place behind each closed cubicle. I noticed an elderly mother surrounded by her family, speaking to her in hushed encouragement. A father sat with his only daughter, who held his hand, tears glistening in her eyes.

A sudden chill ran through me, but then I looked at Bhanu as he was wheeled into the ward. His face was serene, his lips carrying a trace of a smile, and his eyes bright with hope.

I squeezed his hand as a nurse greeted us with a warm, radiant smile, reflecting the sunshine streaming in from the large windows.

"The view from here is nice. I can even see our condo," Bhanu observed, scanning the room. Then, with a playful grin, he added, "Maybe you can just stay home, and we'll wave at each other."

Sitting beside him, I smiled, trying to mask the gnawing anxiety in my chest.

As the chemotherapy drugs began coursing through his veins, Bhanu remained in good spirits, chatting with the nurses, asking their names, about their families, their work. He even exchanged jokes with them, making the sterile hospital room feel momentarily lighter.

Six hours later, the first part of the chemotherapy cycle was complete. Bhanu was transferred from the Oncology Ward to a regular ward, where the remaining portion of his treatment, an infusion that would last 42 hours, would continue.

At the end of the cycle, we both sat in quiet anticipation, waiting for the dreaded side effects to appear.

"How do you feel?" I asked.

"I'm okay. No problem at all," Bhanu said. "Just the usual, a little nausea and mucus buildup."

The oncologist came to check on him. "You took the first chemo quite well," he said with a nod of approval.

"You can go home now."

But Bhanu hesitated. "We've decided to stay another night, just in case I experience any extreme side effects later."

That night, he slept soundly. The side effects never came.

The next morning, relieved and hopeful, we packed our bags and returned home.

Inside our condominium, near the large window facing the sunroom, we had a small indoor garden. After the first chemo, Bhanu made it his morning ritual to water the plants. He delighted in their freshness, in the deep green of their leaves, in the tiny new sprouts unfurling toward the light.

Over the next few days, Bhanu remained in good spirits -- taking selfies, texting friends, relaxing in his favorite armchair, browsing online -- as if nothing has changed. Each small act -- facing the camera, tapping the keyboard -- seemed like an act of defiance. His way of telling the world: *I'm still here.*

One afternoon, as I stood in the kitchen preparing dinner, he called out, "Do you need anything?"

I barely looked up. "No, I don't need anything. I'm good," I replied absent-mindedly.

Later, when the delivery arrived, I was surprised to find he had ordered a nightshirt for me.

At the time, I thought nothing of it.

I did not know it would be the last thing he would ever buy for me.

When January passed in relative calm, we stepped into February with cautious optimism. Yet an unshakable dread lingered -- cancer hung over us like a storm cloud, heavy and waiting to break.

We were living on borrowed time, bracing for the inevitable.

Chapter Three
February: A Time of Persistence

"Though wise men at their end know dark is right,
Because their words had forked no lightning they
Do not go gentle into that good night."
-Dylan Thomas, *"Do Not Go Gentle into That Good Night"*

2nd chemo, February 13

Three months earlier, when Bhanu was diagnosed with terminal pancreatic cancer, he told his friends he had accepted his fate. But he did not want to leave me alone.

Beating cancer to live longer became his north star. When he experienced only mild side effects after the first chemotherapy cycle, he was eager to have the second scheduled in the second week of February.

"Good news!" his beaming oncologist met us before Bhanu started his second chemotherapy cycle.

"Your CA is now down to 80,000 U/ml. That is more than 50 per cent lower than before you had your first chemo."

The good news lifted Bhanu's spirits. He was relaxed, hopeful, and cheerful as the cancer-fighting drugs coursed through his veins for the next 42 hours.

For a full day, there were no signs of side effects. We went to sleep relieved, believing his body was adjusting to the chemo.

But in the dead of night, the illusion shattered when he woke up with severe diarrhea. The smell hit me before I fully registered what had happened. The sheets were soaked, the floor smeared.

Frantically, he called the nurses. They rushed and cleaned him up while a cleaning lady wiped the floor and deodorized the room.

"I am sorry for the mess and for waking you up in the middle of the night, darling," he said shakily.

I felt someone just stabbed my heart as I looked at my husband's embarrassed face. His eyes were downcast, apologetic, stripped of dignity.

"It is alright. It is not your fault. It's the chemo," I said gently, trying to comfort him while fighting back my tears. "Go back to sleep now. You still have twelve hours before you finish the treatment."

Exhausted, we both slept fitfully the rest of the night.

Despite the night's ordeal, fifteen hours later Bhanu was fit to go home. He left the hospital with quiet determination, still holding on to his north star.

For a couple of days, things were quiet, though Bhanu often struggled with pain, nausea, and mucus buildup.

Gone were the moments of lightheartedness, his jokes, the twinkle in his eyes.

With almost no appetite, Bhanu subsisted on his daily dose of bits of boiled potatoes, half a boiled egg, and a few spoonsful of chicken soup.

One day, hoping to change his diet, I ordered cream of mushroom soup for lunch. To our delight, Bhanu loved it. He finished almost the entire bowl.

"I think this is good for you," I said, hopeful. "Would you like to have it again for dinner?"

He nodded enthusiastically.

That night, we were relieved when he ate with gusto.

"Good, isn't it?" I asked as he set his spoon down.

"Yes, it was good," he said, pushing back his chair to stand.

But before he could even finish his sentence, his face twisted in pain. He clutched his stomach, retched, and suddenly vomited, spilling everything down his chest and onto the floor.

"No, no, please, God, no," I wanted to scream. Instead, I stood there helplessly as he tried to wipe himself off, his hands trembling.

My heart raced. He must be so hungry. He was already so thin, and now, after finally managing to eat a substantial meal, he had lost it all.

"I'm sorry, darling," he murmured, his voice small, his face full of unspoken suffering.

"It's all right," I said, swallowing my sorrow. "I'll give you some Ensure before bed."

That was all I could manage. I wanted to say more, to comfort him, to take away his suffering. But inside, my heart was breaking.

Bhanu waved me away and slowly rose to his feet, his back still straight, his head still held high. He walked with dignity to our bed, but I could not stop staring at his legs. They have become much thinner, brittle, like dry branches. I was afraid they might snap.

In the days leading up to his third chemotherapy session, I racked my brain for ways to increase his food intake.

"Should I order ramen?" I asked one evening, hoping to tempt his appetite. "I know how much you like it."

"Yes, yes," he said eagerly, happy for something different. That night, we enjoyed our dinner, savoring a rare moment of normalcy, and went to bed hoping for peaceful sleep.

But in the middle of the night, I woke with a start. Bhanu was moving quietly toward the bathroom, one hand on the wall for support.

"Darling, what's wrong?" I asked, immediately following him.

"My stomach is bad. Sorry, I didn't mean to wake you."

"It's okay to wake me up," I whispered, helping him sit on the toilet, trying to keep my voice steady.

After cleaning him up, I gave him anti-diarrheal medicine and guided him back to bed, praying his stomach would settle.

Sometime before dawn, I stirred again. Bhanu was out of bed, moving toward the door. His soiled shorts were scattered across the floor.

"Oh no, not again," I thought. "Darling, where are you going?"

"I don't want to disturb you, so I'm moving to the sunroom," he said, almost a whisper.

"You have to wake me if you need the bathroom," I said, half-annoyed, half-heartbroken. I knew he was trying to spare me, but I wished he would not.

By morning, I called his oncologist.

"Let's try another medication," the doctor advised. "If it doesn't work, bring him to the hospital."

The new medicine seemed to help - Bhanu did not go to the toilet all morning. Relieved, I prepared our lunch, trying to ignore the gnawing worry in my chest.

"It's Ensure time," I announced cheerfully as I entered the sunroom.

But my smile faded when I saw him. His own smile was nervous, sheepish, the kind a child might give after being caught misbehaving.

"Darling, I'm very sorry," he murmured, his voice trembling in embarrassment. He tried to cover the mess on the bed, as if he could hide his suffering from me.

"It's okay," I said gently. "But you should have called me to help you."

"You were busy," he said softly.

"I'm here for you," I reminded him, helping him to his feet.

As we made our way to the bathroom, his body betrayed him again.

"Oh no... no," he gasped. His anguished eyes shone with unshed tears. "I'm so sorry, darling."

"Don't worry about it," I said, though my own voice wavered. Inside, I felt as if I were walking a tightrope -- supporting Bhanu with my weak left arm and gripping my walking stick with my right, while trying to avoid stepping into the mess on the floor.

After I cleaned him up, I called the oncologist again.

"Let's observe for now," the doctor said. "If it gets worse, bring him in."

Bhanu spent the rest of the afternoon in bed, silent, exhausted, ashamed. I busied myself washing the soiled bedcovers, scrubbing the sunroom, and preparing dinner. Work and worry helped me forget the reality of being hemiplegic.

For a few hours, things seemed stable. But by nightfall, the diarrhea returned with a vengeance. The nausea worsened. So did the mucus buildup in his throat.

I knew what I had to do. Again.

I packed our bags and called an ambulance.

In the emergency room, the doctor ordered a round of tests.

"He doesn't have a bacterial infection this time," he said after reviewing the initial results. "We're not sure what's causing the diarrhea. He'll need to be admitted. We'll keep him in the ICU for observation."

The routine was all too familiar now. Bhanu gets sick. Call the ambulance. Emergency room. Admission. ICU.

By the time I finished the paperwork, it was past 9 p.m. I had not eaten dinner, but I felt a quiet relief knowing Bhanu was in the hands of professionals.

"Be careful on your way home," Bhanu said, his concern for me shining through his exhaustion. "Ask the guard downstairs to get a taxi for you. Have him write down the registration plate."

"Don't worry," I told him, forcing a brave smile. "I'll be all right."

Back in our condominium, the silence was suffocating. The place felt hollow, stripped of warmth, as if it were holding its breath, waiting to exhale.

Shadows danced across the living room, and in the stillness, I imagined the malignant eyes of cancer watching me from the darkness, an unrelenting presence I could not escape.

I hurried to our bedroom and flicked on the light. There, hanging on the wall, was a poster of "The Dream", Henri Rousseau's painting.

Bhanu had bought it forty years ago, back when we were graduate students in Baltimore. It depicted a naked woman reclining on a lounge chair in the middle of a lush, dreamlike jungle, surrounded by wild animals gazing at her in quiet admiration.

Bhanu had loved it so much that we hung it in our apartment's living room, a centerpiece of our shared space. When we finished our studies a year later, we shipped it to Bangkok, where it took its place in the bedroom of our first home.

And now, it was here in our condominium, a silent witness to the joy we had once known and now, to the most devastating chapter of our lives.

I stared at the painting, longing to slip into its world, to be that woman -- untouched by grief, far from this reality where every moment was a reminder of Bhanu's pain and suffering.

At dawn, I was awakened by a call from Bhanu's physician. He was stable enough to be moved to a regular room, but he would need to stay in the hospital a few more days for additional tests and treatments.

His colon was fine, but once again, a bacterial infection had taken hold, most likely from the ramen we had eaten.

The chemotherapy had weakened his immune system, leaving him defenseless against even the smallest threats. His red blood cell count had dropped too low, and he needed a transfusion.

Four days later, when his condition improved, his oncologist suggested, "Since you're already here, why don't we move up your third round of chemo by two days?"

We agreed.

3rd chemo, February 25

Before each chemotherapy session, Bhanu had to undergo a series of lab tests: blood, urine, thyroid, protein, and more.

By the third session, his body had already begun to wear down. His once strong arm now looked frail as the lab technician searched for a vein. He did not flinch when the needle went in, his face carefully expressionless. But his eyes betrayed him, a quiet mix of pain and determination.

The oncologist, his voice gentle but steady, reviewed the latest results. "Your protein and red blood cell count are low," he said matter-of-factly.

Then, after a measured pause, he added, "Your carbohydrate antigen has risen again -- from 80,000 to 100,000. Likely due to the recent infection."

I felt my heart skip a bit, the words sounding like thunder. Without thinking, I reached for Bhanu's hands, rubbing warmth into them as if I could somehow shield him from the news.

I turned away so he would not see my eyes. He squeezed my hand, firm, reassuring, as if it were me who needed comforting.

"Alright," he said, his voice steady, even light. "Let's get started."

The third chemotherapy session passed without complications. The side effects -- diarrhea, loss of appetite -- were manageable. Forty-two hours later, we were finally discharged.

Exhausted but steady, Bhanu's thoughts, as always, were on me.

The taxi line outside was long, stretching down the sidewalk. I told him to wait while I ran to the bathroom. When I returned, I scanned the crowd, expecting to see him standing where I had left him.

Instead, I spotted him inside a sleek black limousine, waving at me from the back seat.

I rushed over, impressed but at the same time worried. "This is expensive!"

He smiled, reaching for my hand as I slid in beside him. "Yes, it is," he admitted. "But I don't want you waiting surrounded by all these people. Who knows? They might have Covid."

I let out a breath of a laugh, shaking my head. Even now, after everything, he was still looking out for me.

After the third chemotherapy cycle, its side effects were taking their toll. Bhanu became weaker, the pain more constant but he never let it show. I never heard him groan or cry out. Not a whimper, not a stifled gasp of agony, just the briefest flicker of anguish across his face before he forced it away.

"It's the bad guy again attacking me, darling," he said, managing a bitter smile.

Later, the illness had taken another cruel turn -- he had become incontinent.

"That's the fifth time this afternoon," I said gently while helping him clean up. "We're going to run out of pants and underwear."

I hesitated before adding, "I think you should wear adult diapers."

His expression tightened. "Can I not wear them?" he asked, his voice barely above a whisper. "It makes me feel like an infant."

I reached for his hand. "I know," I said. "But it would save me a lot of time washing your pants."

For a moment, he just looked at me, his eyes shadowed with pity. Not for himself, but for me.

"Okay, darling," he said finally. "I'll do it."

As we struggled to fasten the diaper in place, I could feel his humiliation, his quiet resignation. So, this is what it has come to, he must have been thinking.

The days passed in a blur of pain, exhaustion, and slow decline. The bad guy came at all hours, unrelenting. Diarrhea, mucus buildup, and his inability to eat more than a few bites of food drained what little strength he had left.

He stopped taking selfies. He barely spoke. He shut off the Buddhist chants he once listened to for comfort.

Sometimes, he would sit in the sunroom, staring into nothing. Other times, he would lie in bed, eyes shut, pretending to sleep because real sleep never came.

And yet, through it all, he kept trying.

Determined, despite the agony, he would push himself out of bed, walk a few slow, unsteady steps to the dining table, rest for a moment, then walk back. A minute of rest. Then he would do it again. And again. Until exhaustion finally won.

One afternoon, during a rare moment of quiet, he turned to me.

"I'll transfer funds to your account so you can pay the hospital next time," he said.

I nodded inattentively. "That's good. But I can always use my own."

"No," he said firmly. "Keep your money for rainy days."

A while later, his expression changed. "Bad news, darling."

I tensed. "What's wrong?"

His lips pressed together. "I… I forgot my account number," he said, his voice laced with frustration.

He sat there for a long moment, brows furrowed, fingers tapping absently against his phone. I could see the struggle in his face, the quiet panic of something slipping just out of reach.

Then, suddenly, his eyes lit up.

"Great! I remember it now!" he announced triumphantly.

We both let out a breath, half laugh, half relief. Even now, even with everything, he still found small victories to celebrate.

To Love and to Hold

You don't shower any more, darling," I said one night after dinner.

"It's painful," he murmured, barely audible.

"Then I'll sponge bath you," I said while feeling a sharp tug in my heart.

And so, our nightly ritual began.

Bhanu exhaled deeply as I wiped his face, ears, and neck with a warm, soapy cloth. "That feels so good," he murmured, closing his eyes.

"This is the best time of the day for me," he sighed, relaxing into the warmth of my hands. But as I moved the cloth down his arms and chest, I felt how thin he had become.

His ribs, sharp and bony, jutted beneath his skin. His arms were frail, his flesh barely there, just a fraction of the man he once was. The image seared into me. He looked like the emaciated prisoners in concentration camps in World War II photographs, bodies reduced to shadows of their former selves.

I had never imagined Bhanu would resemble them.

A lump rose in my throat, and my eyes burned. I blinked rapidly, fighting away the tears, and hurried to finish. I smoothed lotion over his fragile skin, dressed him in freshly ironed pajamas, and arranged the pillows so he could breathe easily.

Finally, I leaned in to hug him.

But he gently pushed me away.

"I am sorry, darling," he said, his voice thick with sadness. "My chest hurts when pressed."

Stung, I pulled back quickly, as if I was burned. "All right, sleep now," I said, straining to keep my voice steady. "I'll take a shower and join you."

Maybe he did not want me to hold him because he could no longer hold me back. I had seen him struggle to lift his arms.

Still, he reached for my hand. His fingers, though weak, pressed against mine. "That's the trouble," he said, a wistful smile on his lips. "You love me too much."

I felt as if someone had just slashed my heart. I did not know what to say or do, except ran to the bathroom as quickly as I could.

In the shower, I finally let the tears flow freely, sobs wracking my body as the water drowned out the sound.

I thought of Bhanu's shrunken frame, the weight of his suffering, the tenderness in his eyes even as he pulled away. It felt as if the wound in my heart would never stop bleeding.

"What kept you so long?" Bhanu said softly when I finally joined him in bed, thankful the lights were dim. He could not see my red eyes.

"I wanted to smell nice for you," I said, pretending to sound happy.

"Yes, you do smell nice," he said, reaching for my hand.

I held his hand for a minute then gently placed it on the pillow next to me. "I'm going to pray the rosary now," I said.

"Pray for me," he murmured.

"I do. Every night."

"Why don't we pray together?" I asked.

"Let's start tomorrow," he whispered.

The following night, after his sponge bath, I sat next to him on the edge of the bed. Our fingers intertwined as we prayed the rosary. Bhanu closed his eyes, his face peaceful, his breathing slow.

Thus, praying the rosary became part of our nightly ritual.

Bhanu was a Buddhist, but after four decades of marriage to me, a Catholic, he had come to embrace the traditions of my faith. He eagerly decorated the Christmas tree with me, scoured the city for poinsettias, and drove me to Christmas Eve Mass.

On Palm Sunday, he carefully preserved the blessed fronds, and during Lent, he reminded me to avoid meat on Fridays. Each Easter, he happily took home bottles of holy water, treating them with the same reverence I did.

But above all, the sacrament that meant the most to him was marriage.

When we first wed in 1979, it was not in a church. We simply registered our marriage at a district office in Bangkok -- just the two of us and a pair of witnesses. No vows before God, no grand ceremony.

That changed twenty-five years later.

I had suffered a hemorrhagic stroke, severe enough that my friends feared I would not survive. As I lay in a hospital bed, weak and disoriented, they called for a Catholic priest to administer the Last Rites -- the sacrament given to the dying for spiritual strength and preparation for the afterlife.

But as a Catholic, I had never been married in the church. According to its teachings, I had been "living in sin" all these years. And so, before the Last Rites could be performed, my friends hastily arranged a Catholic wedding.

In that small hospital room, with my hair unkempt and my mouth slightly misshapen from the stroke, I lay in bed as a priest officiated our marriage. Bhanu stood beside me, solemn and steadfast, as we exchanged our vows:

"I, Bhanupong, take you, Divina, for my lawful wedded wife, to love and to hold, from this day forward, for better or for worse, for richer or poorer, in sickness and in health, till death do us part."

(And I said the same.)

At last, our union had the Church's blessing.

The words must have etched themselves into Bhanu's heart. The very next day, at his nephew's Buddhist wedding, he was asked to speak about marriage. Standing before the guests, he simply repeated the words of our vow.

"Darling," he later told me with a chuckle, "everyone thought I was such a devoted husband, such an expert on marriage. But I only told them what it truly means -- to love and to hold."

And he lived those words every day.

At night, after prayers, I would leave him to tidy up the kitchen or finish the ironing. It was often an hour before I returned to bed.

"Why are you still awake?" I would ask.

"I'm waiting for you," he would reply.

I would slip under the covers, reach for his hand, and he would squeeze mine gently.

Then we would sleep, until the pain woke him again.

Until he could no longer hold my hand.

Until love was all that remained.

Chapter Four
March: Shattered Hope

"Hope is a strange invention -
A Patent of the Heart-
In unremitting action.
Yet never wearing out."
- Emily Dickinson, "Hope is a Strange Invention"

4th Chemo, March 6

As in previous chemotherapy sessions, Bhanu had to have his blood tested first. As the technician prepared the needle, he extended his thin arm without hesitation. His face remained impassive, his eyes distant, masking the pain as the needle pierced his vein.

"Good news!" his oncologist greeted us before Bhanu's fourth round of chemo. "Your carbohydrate antigen level has dropped again -- from 100,000 to 40,000 U/ml."

The treatment proceeded as planned, but the aftermath remained the same: nausea, mucus buildup, a vanishing appetite. Sleep came in fragments, interrupted by discomfort, by the need to spit out mucus, by quiet calls to the nurse for a urinal or a slow, painful trip to the bathroom.

And always, there was the pain.

Before we left for home the next day, Bhanu's chief physician stopped by.

"You need to eat more," he advised. "You're underweight, undernourished. You need strength for the next cycle. Eat anything you like -- cakes, cookies, even ice cream."

The next day at home, I ordered ice cream and served it after lunch, which Bhanu had barely touched.

"Darling, your doctor said you could eat anything. Even ice cream," I said, handing him a cup of peach-flavored ice cream.

"Yes," he replied glumly, lifting a spoonful to his lips. I watched as he swallowed, his throat twisting to force it down. After just two bites, he put down the spoon and slowly rose from the table.

"That's all you're going to eat?" I asked, my voice dripping with disappointment. "It's very expensive ice cream, you know. And you used to love it."

Bhanu looked at me, his eyes pleading for understanding.

"I can't eat it," he said softly. "Not because I don't like it. My throat hurts too much."

His words felt like a knife twisting in my heart. It was the first time he had voiced his suffering so plainly.

"Come, let me help you to bed," I offered.

"No, I can do it. Finish your ice cream. I know you love it." His voice was heavy with sorrow. He turned and walked away, his steps slow and weighted.

I stared down at the melting ice cream, and suddenly, I was somewhere else. Los Baños, Philippines, September 1978.

It had been a month since Bhanu had given me an orange, and we had begun meeting regularly, talking for hours, exploring the town, sharing meals by the lake.

"We see the world the same way," Bhanu had marveled one evening after a violin concert. "We understand each other completely. Isn't that something? Two complete strangers?"

"Yes," I agreed, "despite our completely different backgrounds."

He hesitated then, wanting to say something more but struggling to find the words. The days of his training were slipping away, and soon, he would be leaving.

Desperate, he sought advice from a Filipina classmate.

"Mininda, how do Filipinos tell someone how they feel?"

"Don't give her flowers or anything like that. Buy her ice cream instead," she advised.

So, two days before my 22nd birthday, Bhanu arrived at my boarding house with a half-gallon of peach-flavored ice cream. Over each melting spoonful, we promised that no matter what happened, we would spend our lives together.

That was 44 years ago. And now, I sat alone, watching peach-flavored ice cream dissolving drip by drip in quiet surrender.

Later that afternoon, I brought Bhanu a glass of Ensure. He sat on the bed, facing the wall.

"I've asked a lawyer to draft my will," he said quietly.

I hesitated, then began massaging his back in silence. In January, I had cautiously brought up the idea of a will, but he had brushed it off. "There's no need for that now. It's too early," he said.

Back then, he had still believed the chemotherapy would buy him years.

Now, two months later, the optimism was gone, swallowed by pain, by nausea, by the relentless loss of appetite.

"Are you afraid?" I asked, my voice a mixture of sympathy and anguish. I kept massaging his back, aching to pull him into my arms, to hold him tight enough to keep him here.

"No, everybody dies," he replied without looking at me. His voice was gentle and soft, almost a whisper. Then he reached for my hand and squeezed it.

I wanted to say, "What about me? I don't know how to live without you." But I swallowed the words, afraid that if I spoke, I would break. Afraid of adding to his suffering.

"I'm going to leave you everything," he said, turning to face me. His eyes were weary but resolute. Then, he lay down and closed his eyes, pretending to sleep.

Outside, the afternoon sun shone brightly, but inside, the day felt dark and cruel.

That night, Bhanu could not sleep.

"The pain is worse," he admitted.

"Why don't you take the liquid morphine?" I asked gently.

"I'm afraid I'll hallucinate," he said, spitting mucus into a bedpan.

I hesitated. Then, standing, I said, "I'll get you some warm milk. Maybe it will help."

"Not too warm," he said. "It would hurt my throat."

In the kitchen, I prepared the milk and, hesitating only for a moment, added 5 mg of liquid morphine.

When I handed it to him, I forced a smile. "Here, I hope it's the right temperature."

He drank it all.

"It's good," Bhanu said after a moment. Then he paused. "But it's a bit sweet."

I pretended not to hear him.

Soon, he was asleep.

At breakfast the next morning, I tried to sound cheerful. "You slept well last night."

"The warm milk helped," he admitted. "But I had strange dreams."

I hesitated before confessing, "I... added morphine."

He looked at me sharply. "Don't do that again."

"I just wanted you to sleep," I said, my voice breaking.

"I know." He said full of understanding.

Five days before his fifth chemotherapy, his will was ready. With our friend Ajarn Nui and our condominium manager as witnesses, Bhanu took the pen with unsteady fingers and signed his name.

As soon as it was done, he returned to bed, speaking little except to whisper his thanks to the witnesses.

By now, his body had withered into a fragile echo of itself -- his cheeks were hollow, his legs narrowed to the length of his bone, no more than scaffolding beneath the skin. Dark circles rimmed his eyes, deepened by sleepless nights and the poison of chemotherapy.

A haunted look had settled on his face -- exhaustion, resignation, and quiet suffering had taken root there.

Still, every day, he forced himself to walk. From our bed to the sunroom and back. A few steps, maybe a dozen. Small, slow, tentative. As if at any moment, his body might betray him.

Still, he walked.

Because Bhanu had never been one to surrender.

And all I could do was watch.

5ᵗʰChemo, March 20

As Bhanu grew weaker, his resolve only became stronger. He could hardly wait for the next round of chemotherapy, his fifth.

That morning, we arrived at the hospital earlier than usual, a mix of dread and anticipation swirling between us. Today, the oncologist would assess the progress of the treatment. After the usual blood tests, Bhanu had a CT scan.

The waiting seemed endless, as I sat next to Bhanu holding his hands in the ambulatory room. When the oncologist finally walked in, my heart pounded. His usual warm smile was absent. He stood next to Bhanu's bed, shuffled his legs a bit, cleared his throat then delivered the results.

The scan results are… mixed," he began carefully. "There are some positive signs. The tumor in the pancreas had shrunk a little from 5.9 centimeters to 5.3 centimeters. The size of peritoneal metastasis decreased slightly. There was no change in the size of umbilical metastasis. There was a reduction in lung nodules. There was no change in the size of adrenal gland metastasis. And the bulbosity of the osteolytic metastasis at the tenth rib decreased.

He took a deep breath. I gripped Bhanu's hands tighter.

"But the carbohydrate antigen went up by 3,000 U/ml from 40,000; it is 43,000."

Then, the final blow: "There are several new lesions in the right hepatic lobe. The cancer has spread to the liver."

The world seemed to have stopped. I dared not look at Bhanu. Afraid that he might see the depth of despair in my eyes. The room fell silent and cold.

Bhanu stared at the ceiling for a long moment, then turned to me. I wanted to hold him, comfort him, shield him from the crushing weight of the results.

"I suggest to continue the chemotherapy. We will have to re-formulate the drugs," the oncologist broke the deafening silence. "We have to adjust the drug regimen." He was throwing us a lifeline.

"We are supposed to transfer to Thammasat University after this assessment," I said, my voice distant, as if someone else were speaking.

"We will have the fifth chemotherapy here," Bhanu said, his tone steady, emotionless.

The oncologist nodded, "I will order new formulation for your therapy today," the oncologist said.

"Have your breakfast now," Bhanu told me when the doctor left us to ourselves.

"I'll eat later," I murmured. I could barely process what just happened.

During the chemotherapy session, Bhanu mostly slept. He no longer chatted or joked with the nurses, preferring solitude and rest. If he was disappointed with the assessment, he did not show it.

That night, as the drugs coursed through his veins, he turned to me and said, "I will hire a special nurse to stay with me tonight so you can rest."

Even in exhaustion, even in the face of devastating news, he was thinking of me.

"We don't need a special nurse. I'll take care of you. I am okay," I replied. I sat beside him, watching his face. So tired, yet so determined. Even now, he was still fighting.

And I would be there, fighting beside him.

As in previous chemotherapy treatments, Bhanu was transferred to a regular room after the first six hours of the treatment cycle. There he would continue the chemotherapy for 40 hours before returning home.

During this time, his chief physician came to visit.

"He needs to have a blood transfusion when he finishes the chemo. His blood count is way below normal. And he still lacks the necessary nutrients to give him strength," his voice was insistent.

When the chemotherapy ended around nine in the morning, Bhanu remained in bed for another six hours, receiving blood.

While he lay there, I went to a bank at the hospital's basement where Bhanu had an account. I filled out a withdrawal slip, brought it to him to sign, and then returned to the bank and handed it to a teller.

"We can't process this. The signature did not match our record," the teller said curtly. Frustrated, I ran back to Bhanu's room. Breathless, I told him what happened.

Fortunately, the oncologist was around. He volunteered to write a note: "Patient has advanced pancreatic cancer that altered his handwriting,"

I did not go back to the bank. Bhanu was finishing his transfusion, and soon we would be going home.

At least, that was the plan.

But at 3 p.m., as I gathered our things, Bhanu barely moved. His limbs were leaden, his voice faint.

"I don't feel well, darling," he murmured. "I will stay another night."

"Good," I said forcing a smile. "And I don't have to make you my lousy chicken soup."

He managed a weak chuckle.

A nurse checked his vitals. "Low grade fever," she said. "We'll give him antibiotics."

Rupture

By early evening, Bhanu's throat had clogged with mucus again. He picked at his dinner. He sipped some soup, nibbled on fruit, and pushed the rest away.

At 7:30 p.m., while I was helping Bhanu take antibiotics, to my horror I saw something coming out of his mouth.

Something black.

At first, my mind refused to comprehend what I was seeing. A strange darkness, thick, unnatural pooling in his throat. I caught my breath. I thought, "No! It can't be.... Is that..."

Then he retched.

A torrent of blood spilled from his mouth, coating his chin, his neck, his chest, the sheets. For a moment, sheer terror enveloped me.

"Oh, no! No! No!! What is happening? Oh, God, what is happening?" I heard myself crying. My hands shaking, searching for something -- anything -- to stop the bleeding.

The nurse's aide stood frozen, petrified.

"Get a bed pan, quick!" I yelled, but she did not move.

The blood kept coming. Thick, dark, unstoppable.

Running footsteps pounded down the hall as nurses rushed in. One grabbed a towel, another called for emergency assistance. But nothing stopped the flow. It was flowing like a waterfall, a rupture. A merciless tide.

Bhanu lay still. He must have been terrified. He had always hated the sight of blood, but his face showed only quiet resignation. His eyes met mine. They were full of apology. "What have I put you through?" They seemed to say.

"Where is the doctor?" I screamed. "We're in a hospital. Why isn't anyone helping my husband?"

Finally, the head nurse arrived. "The oncologist ordered a transfer to the ICU."

Within moments, the emergency team rushed Bhanu away while other nurses hurried to gather our things. I followed in a daze going through the familiar motions of ICU paperwork, though my hands were barely moving. My mind was blank.

My mind and my heart were in turmoil. I did not know how serious was Bhanu's bleeding. I desperately wanted to know how he was feeling. Was he in pain? Was he terribly frightened?

He hardly said a word since he was transferred to the ICU. His forlorn and tired eyes followed my every move.

It was past midnight when I finished signing the ICU formalities. When I left, Bhanu did not say his usual "goodbye" or "be careful". For a moment, he just looked at me sadly, then closed his eyes.

A couple of young nurses, their faces soft with sympathy, helped me find a taxi. The night seemed so still, as if holding its breath as I sat inside the taxi, exhausted and still shaken. The memory of Bhanu's blood -- dark, endless -- played in my mind.

As I entered our condo, I was struck by its tranquility. It felt untouched by the horror I just witnessed a few hours ago. But as I stepped into our dark bedroom, something had changed. I sensed the scepter of death, once distant, now lengthened like the sharpened tip of a blade, hovering above us.

Still, I clung to hope. Clung to the thought that Bhanu would be spared. For just a little longer.

Completely drained, I collapsed into sleep, only to be woken early by a call from Bhanu's chief physician.

Because of Who He Was

"We ran several tests last night but there is no indication that your husband has infection. We recommend that he undergo gastroscopy today. You have to come to the hospital to sign the consent form as the next of kin," he said.

After signing the paperwork, I went to the bank to withdraw from Bhanu's account. I presented the withdrawal slip that he signed along with the note from his oncologist. The bank manager hardly glanced at the paper.

"We cannot accept this. The signature did not match our record," she simply repeated what the teller said yesterday.

Frustration surged through me. "You did not even bother to read the doctor's note," I snapped, my voice raising. My eyes fell on the bank's poster nearby: "*We are here to serve you*".

"Look at your poster! You are a bunch of liars! You don't serve anyone, you only care about money!" I lashed out, sounding unhinged.

The manager was unmoved. "Under banking regulations, the doctor's note is not acceptable. Only the account owner's signature is valid."

As a former banker, I knew she was right but knowing did not change the fact that I needed money. ICU care and the gastroscopy were costly, and Bhanu's savings were already running low.

Desperate, I called Dr. Naris for assistance. He directed me to Ajarn Preecha, Bhanu's former colleague at Thammasat.

After listening to me, Ajarn Preecha said: "I would call the bank's president. He was your husband's former student."

After what felt like an eternity of back-and-forth discussions, the bank finally found a solution: two branch employees would accompany me to the ICU. There they would witness Bhanu signing the withdrawal slip and take a photograph as verification.

Bhanu was groggy from the sedation, his throat raw and painful, but he nodded when I explained the situation. The bank staff supported his trembling hand as he scrawled his name.

"I'll do it for you, darling," he whispered, his voice barely audible.

Watching Bhanu struggle to sign, I fought back my tears. He looked at me despondently, he realized his savings were dwindling. He had hoped to leave them all to me.

After completing the bank transaction, I wandered to a nearby restaurant. It was past two in the afternoon and I had not eaten the whole day. Drained, and overwhelmed, I took a bite of food, but tears mingled with each mouthful.

The next day, I faced the same battle again -- this time at Thammasat University Cooperative where I needed to withdraw more funds. Once again, my request was denied. Signature did not match.

Thammasat is almost an hour's taxi ride from Bhanu's hospital. The unfamiliar place and uneven footpath made my journey more exhausting. But my mind was not on the logistics. All I could think was Bhanu; his condition was deteriorating each day. He was like a prey being hunted relentlessly, mercilessly. Still, he was defiant but the hunter was closing in.

As I pleaded with Cooperative staff, my voice cracked under the weight of desperation. Then a pair of elderly ladies approached me.

"Who is your husband?" asked one.

I turned. "Ajarn Bhanupong," I answered barely holding back my tears.

The woman's face softened. "Bhanupong! I was his adviser when he was a student here."

Hearing those words, I broke down. I pictured Bhanu as a young man, full of hope, laughter, his future stretching ahead of him, just like the students I had passed by on the way here. But now, his life was slipping away.

"We did not know he was sick. What was his cancer?"

"Pancreatic cancer. Stage 4."

"We have to help him," said Ajarn Chusee, Bhanu's former adviser.

That afternoon, I was not able to get the money I had come for. But for the first time in weeks, I felt less alone. Two strangers had stepped in, offering kindness in a world that had felt unbearably cruel. For a brief moment, I was comforted.

Back at the hospital, Bhanu's chief physician was waiting with the results of the gastroscopy.

"The results are inconclusive," he said. The words landed like a punch, $1,500 for nothing. "Most likely the massive bleeding two nights ago was caused by esophageal varices. Or, it could be the two duodenal ulcers seen during gastroscopy. He also has gastritis.

"Your husband experienced massive drop of red blood cells. He needs blood transfusion. We will move him to a regular room tomorrow."

While he was receiving treatment, Dr. Naris called, urging him to transfer to Thammasat University hospital where about 90 per cent of his medical charges would be subsidized.

At first, Bhanu resisted. He worried about me. The two-hour commute between Thammasat hospital and our condo would be too difficult. Worse, he still remembered his experience four months ago when he had been left unattended for almost eight hours at a public hospital.

But this time, two directors from the hospital personally reached out assuring him that he would be in a private room, that I would be able to stay with him. Bhanu was running out of options, and we both knew it.

Finally, after a long silence, he sighed. "All right," he said. "I will go."

Not for him. But for me.

Leaving Samitivej

As we said goodbye and thanked his oncologist, his chief physician, and the nurses who cared for him over the last four months, a sharp ache rose in my throat. Sadness weighed heavily on me, and beneath it, a quiet sense of misgiving.

I knew Bhanu wanted to stay in this hospital.

Samitivej had become a place of familiarity, of comfort, in the midst of his suffering. He liked the attentive care, the modern facilities, the convenience of being close to our condominium. He was now familiar not only with the doctors and medical staff, but also the cleaning ladies and the wheelchair assistants.

This hospital had been his refuge. And yet, he chose to leave, for me. He decided to move to Thammasat Hospital to secure my life in the future.

On the way home, he barely spoke. His fingers gripped mine tightly, as if drawing strength from our touch.

His silence filled the car, heavier than words ever could.

At home, the sorrow that clung to him did not lift. A shadow of anguish followed him from room to room. Even the arrival of our infant granddaughter, usually the brightest light of his day, did little to stir him.

In the past, he had been eager to play with her, to scoop her in his arms, to press kisses on her soft cheeks. But today, he barely acknowledged her. His smile, when it finally came, was faint, just a slight upturn of his lips.

Instead of engaging, he just lay on the bed, watching her with wary, distant eyes.

By now, the toll of his battle with cancer was undeniable. His once thick dark salt-and-pepper hair had thinned to wisps, now completely white. His fingers, all bones and sharp angles, bore nails that had darkened to near black. His skin, burned from inside by chemotherapy, had taken on an unnatural shade of dark brown. His once handsome face, now hollowed and emaciated, was almost unrecognizable.

And yet, despite it all, his sunken eyes had a flicker of defiance.

Thammasat Hospital - The First Four Days

We spent a day at home before I took Bhanu to Thammasat University Hospital, about an hour's drive from our condo. Ajarn Nui was kind enough to lend us her car and driver for the trip.

The night before, despite his frailty, Bhanu found strength to pack his bag and prepare his clothes for the trip.

Our appointment with the chief oncologist was at nine in the morning, so we got up early. I gave Bhanu a soft-boiled egg and a glass of Ensure. Before leaving, he sat quietly in his favorite armchair, perhaps remembering all those evenings we watched movies together, or the times he rested there to relax after a long day's work. Maybe he was wondering if he would ever sit there again.

Although he could barely walk on his own by now, he insisted on carrying his bag, pressing his arm on the wall of the hallway for support as he walked unassisted to the elevator. Before stepping out, he turned back and gave our bedroom, our home, a long lingering look before closing the door.

As our car moved along the highway to Thammasat University Hospital, Bhanu was mostly silent. He held my hand and looked at me, as if tracing those years we had traveled along this very road, years now etched in the lines on my face.

Our first home had been about half an hour from Thammasat University Hospital. We were just starting out then. We would wake up at five in the morning, take a bus to our work, and return home more than twelve hours later.

A year after we moved, Bhanu bought a second-hand car and began driving me to and from my office, even though it was more than an hour from his.

Two years later, I had my own car, provided by my employer. I was moving up the ranks. We then moved to new places, and built a different life. But now, it felt like we were coming home.

An hour later, we arrived at the hospital - into chaos. The chief oncologist we were supposed to meet was attending a seminar. The hospital's executive director, who had promised Bhanu that he would oversee his admission, was nowhere to be found.

We had no idea where to begin. The admission office was overwhelmed, swarming with patients requesting to be admitted or see a doctor.

Bhanu sat in a wheelchair, watching in quiet resignation as his three university friends helped us navigate the confusion. His expression said it all: "This is exactly what I was afraid would happen."

After more than three exhausting hours, Bhanu was finally admitted -- not to a private room, but to a special unit in the emergency department while we waited for a room to become available.

While there, a group of young oncologists came and asked several questions about Bhanu's health. Fortunately, Bhanu's doctors at Samitivej prepared a CD of his complete cancer treatment history. After a brief conversation, they left.

It was now almost three in the afternoon. Bhanu had not eaten since seven in the morning. If he was starving, he did not say anything. He did not even complain even as mucus accumulated in his throat. His only concern was me. "You haven't had anything either," he said softly.

Finally, at 4 p.m., a private room became available.

It was smaller than Bhanu's room at Samitivej but it felt less stifling. There was a small balcony where I could look at the sky, feel the wind, and watch people from neighboring buildings go about their lives.

That evening, the oncology team visited again. The leader had reviewed Samitivej's report and told us what we already knew: the cancer had spread to Bhanu's liver.

Then, she recommended that Bhanu send his blood sample to a laboratory in the US for genetic analysis. A targeted treatment could then be administered based on his genetic makeup. It was expensive, but at that moment, a sliver of hope broke through the darkness. We agreed.

On his second day at Thammasat University Hospital, Bhanu's mood lifted slightly. He ate a little bit more. The food here was better than at Samitivej. But the mucus, as always, continued tormenting him.

Thammasat Hospital felt like a world away from the bustling city of Bangkok. I was disconnected from everyone I knew. So, when our friend, Ajarn Nui, visited and brought fruits, other snacks, and a much-needed small kettle for me, I was overjoyed. At least, now I could have hot tea or coffee whenever I needed it.

Moving to a Suite

In the early evening of the third day, the chief oncologist finally visited Bhanu. Again, she told us what we already knew: He was severely undernourished. He needed to eat more to regain strength and stamina.

She said a dietician would visit the next day to plan his meals. Until then, chemotherapy would be postponed until he was strong enough.

As if warning us not to have false hope, she repeated what the other doctors had said: the cancer had spread. I was crushed, not only by her words but by the note of resignation in her voice. There was no trace of empathy.

Still reeling from the visit, I helped Bhanu take his medications. As I gave him a dose of liquid medicine, he watched me intently. Then ever so slowly, he raised his right hand -- his movement strained, deliberate -- and gently caressed my cheek.

"You are still my beautiful girl. And I love you," he said softly. "But, why are you very sad?"

I did not know what to say. I had no words that would not break me. I could not tell him that our time together might be short, that I would be completely, utterly lost alone in this world.

"Because… because you ate very little," I said, swallowing hard to steady my voice, forcing back my tears.

Just then, a maid entered to take the food tray. I seized the chance to escape to the bathroom, turning on the shower to drown my sobs. There, as I often did now, I let the tears flow freely.

While in the shower, I heard voices and some commotion outside. I hurriedly dressed. But my weak left leg slowed me down.

By the time I emerged, the room had fallen silent.

Bhanu was gone.

His bed mattress was rolled up.

Panic run through me. "What happened? Where is my husband?"

Just then a nurse came in, smiling.

"Don't worry, Madam. Ajarn has been transferred to another room in another wing of the hospital. We'll take you there."

Relieved, I followed her. Bhanu had been moved to a suite.

At last, he was given a room befitting his years of service at Thammasat University and his tireless efforts to establish another campus outside the city of Bangkok. After years of pushing university officials and the national government, Bhanu helped make the university's Rangsit campus a reality.

Established in early 1990s, it is a sprawling 70.3-hectare campus in Pathum Thani province about 50 kilometers from downtown Bangkok. Today, it accommodates 30,000 students a year, offering courses in all fields including sociology, humanities, health sciences, business, and economics.

Bhanu's suite had a 50-square meter patient room, a dining area with a six-seater dining table, and an adjacent reception space furnished with a sofa set and a TV set. The reception area opened onto a wide balcony overlooking the adjacent buildings and a garden below. There was also a pantry equipped with a nine-foot refrigerator, a microwave oven and a large kettle. Next to it was the bathroom.

"This place is very nice. Do you like it?" I asked, trying to sound cheerful.

Bhanu barely reacted. He was distressed by the constant build-up of mucus in his throat as the nurses changed his clothes.

"Your bed is very small," he finally muttered.

"Don't worry. I'm used to it by now," I said.

Bhanu knew how much I liked sleeping in spacious beds, where I could move like the hands of a clock throughout the night. He used to tease me about it, even taking a picture of me sprawled across the bed as a proof that I encroached on his side.

For the next three days, Bhanu's condition remained unchanged. He ate very little. His sleep was often punctuated by near-hourly visits by the nurses who came to suction the mucus in his throat.

Visiting Muang Ake

While he was at the hospital, I decided to visit our old home in Muang Ake, a gated housing estate just 20 minutes from Thammasat Hospital.

We have not lived there since it was damaged by a massive flood 11 years ago. Over the last few years, Bhanu had worked on renovating and refurbishing it, hoping we could move back soon. But he never had a chance to finish it. First, the Covid-19. Then, cancer.

Our Muang Ake home was a testament to our hard work and dedication to our careers. Mine in banking, Bhanu's in academia.

Fifteen years since returning from our studies in the United States, we were finally able to purchase our second home. It sat on a quiet tree-lined street, across a small pond where pink lilies floated on the water, like a scene from Monet's paintings. Wildflowers framed the footpath and a pair of fruit trees stood guard at the entrance.

But when I arrived this time, my heart sunk.

The pond was no longer clear, covered now with debris and slime. Not a single pink waterlily remained. The wildflowers had withered and the two fruit trees were dead. In their place lay dry leaves and broken branches, like fallen soldiers defeated by the relentless march of time and neglect.

Inside the gate, the sight stung my eyes. The hedges that Bhanu planted and meticulously trimmed were now brittle brown twigs, like tiny skeletons. The once lush grass was gone, replaced by dry, cracked soil that swirled into dust whenever the wind blew. The flower beds where butterflies once danced and the small trees where birds greeted us with their morning songs were bare, lifeless.

I hurried inside, desperate to escape the decay. Here, the traces of Bhanu's renovation were evident. The walls were covered with cream-colored wallpaper. Baby-blue lace curtains adorned the windows. But the emptiness was stark.

The pink floral sofa set that once dominated the living room, facing the French window, was gone. Bhanu and I used to sit there on weekend afternoons admiring our garden, watching butterflies, identifying birds as they flitted by.

Now staring at the vacant space, I could almost hear our voices, talking about nothing and everything, savoring the simple joy of being together.

In the dining room, our six-seater dining table where we had shared countless meals with our son, Tony, was gone, too, destroyed by the flood. I could almost see Tony sitting there, animatedly telling us stories whenever he was home from a boarding school in England.

Adjacent to the dining room was Bhanu's study room where he spent countless hours, reading and researching, surrounded by floor-to-ceiling bookshelves. It was now empty. Like the furniture, the bookshelves had been washed away in the flood. Only a few books we managed to salvage remained upstairs.

As I climbed the stairs, memories came rushing back, especially the first time I attempted this climb six months after my stroke. Bhanu had been right behind me, ready to catch me if I faltered, beaming with pride as I took each slow, determined step. When I finally made it to our bedroom, he was so happy.

On his bedside table, he always kept our framed photograph from New York City. October 2004. He had attended an AEP Meeting at Columbia University. In the photo, he is smiling contentedly as he holds my arm possessively. It was our last trip to New York together. Five months later, I had a stroke. I would never walk normally again.

I remembered those days of recovery. Bhanu had moved his work from his study room downstairs to the small bathroom adjacent to our bedroom, just to be close to me at night. He did not want the bedroom light disturbing my sleep, but he still had research to do, papers to grade, projects to complete.

To this day, I still don't know how he managed it all -- his demanding teaching job, his research, and his travels while taking care of me.

Every morning before he left for work, he made me breakfast. On his way home from work, he stopped at the supermarket, then cooked dinner.

At least three times during the week, he would take me to the hospital for my cardiology check-ups and my therapy sessions. And when emergencies struck in the middle of the night, he was the one who rushed me to the hospital.

Things eased slightly when I went back to work five years later. But still, Bhanu drove me to my office, then picked me up in the evening. He continued to prepare my breakfast and dinner, run errands, and shop for our needs, as our maid only cleaned the house and did the laundry.

Then came the floods. We moved to the city where our condominium was too small to accommodate a live-in helper. Bhanu learned to do the laundry, mend my clothes, roll my hair, and, amazingly, improve his cooking.

And he continued being my driver. He did it all happily and cheerfully, without a single word of complaint.

During the height of the Covid-19 pandemic, we were together almost 24 hours a day, every day. And now, he is in the hospital fighting for his life. I had no idea how to navigate life without him by my side.

Before leaving Muang Ake, I checked the kitchen. Even here, the room that Bhanu renovated first, held traces of his thoughtfulness. He installed a state-of-the art oven because he knew how much I loved to bake.

Even though Bhanu's cancer had metastasized to his liver, I still clung to hope. I prayed that the lab results would reveal markers that would allow the oncology team to administer a targeted treatment.

And so, I began making plans.

I would convert part of the living room into Bhanu's bedroom, complete with a hospital bed, an oxygen tank, and whatever medical equipment he might need. His bed would face the French windows opening out to the garden.

I would have the gardener plant fresh grass to cover the barren soil. I would replace the hedges, and plant bougainvillea.

I imagined pushing Bhanu in a wheelchair, letting him soak in the morning sun and listen to the birds sing. We would laugh at our silly jokes, just as we always did.

I knew his condition was precarious, and time was slipping away. But I refused to give up.

I wanted his remaining days to be happy.

Chapter Five
April: The Descent of Twilight

"Now fades the glimmering landscape on the sight
And all the air a solemn stillness holds,"
- *Thomas Gray, "Elegy Written in a Country Churchyard"*

When Silence Began, April 5

Two days after my visit to Muang Ake was Easter Sunday, a day of rebirth and new hope.

Our friend, Lucia, arranged for a Catholic priest to visit Bhanu and pray with him. She believed that even though Bhanu was not Catholic, receiving the blessings of the Church would still be meaningful.

Around one o'clock in the afternoon, Father Erasto of the Xaverian Missionaries arrived. Because Bhanu was not Catholic, he could not receive the Last Sacraments. Instead, standing near his bed, we prayed for his health, for his life, for a miracle.

That night, the mucus buildup in Bhanu's throat worsened. It clogged his airway so frequently that I had to call the nurse almost every half an hour to suck it out.

The pattern repeated through the night, relentless, until around dawn when the congestion finally seemed to ease and we both managed to sleep.

At seven, we woke up when the internal medicine doctor made his rounds. I told him about the worsening mucus, but he dismissed it as nothing serious. He repeated the now standard advice: Bhanu needed to eat more.

When the doctor left, I helped Bhanu with breakfast.

"I am very sorry, darling. I kept you awake the whole night," he said weakly, searching my face.

"I'm fine," I reassured him, though my voice wavered. "It is you I'm worried about. You hardly slept last night and now you're eating almost nothing."

I fought back tears as I took in how frail he looked, how weak he had become.

"You should drink that special milk the doctor gave us yesterday," I said, trying to sound hopeful. "He told me that if you can't eat much, the milk will give you nourishment."

"I don't like it," Bhanu said.

"Please just drink it," I pleaded. "You need your strength. If you get stronger, your chemotherapy can resume. (He was supposed to have his next chemotherapy session the next day if his condition was better).

"Please, please, darling." I begged him.

He sighed. "Okay. I'll drink it."

I handed him the glass of milk, watching him anxiously as he drank every last drop.

"How was it?" I asked gladly.

"It was good," Bhanu replied, smiling.

No sooner had he finished than the nightmare began again. He threw up. The milk spilled all over his newly-changed hospital gown, and onto his fresh bedsheets.

"Oh, my God, not again!" I said, "I will call the nurse to change your gown and the bedsheet."

But Bhanu did not respond. His hands flew to his throat, his fingers clutching his skin. His breathing grew labored. He looked at me, his eyes widened in panic. He was gasping for breath.

A nurse rushed in, but Bhanu's condition deteriorated so rapidly that she called a backup. Within seconds, more nurses flooded the room.

I stood beside Bhanu helplessly until one of the nurses gently guided me toward the sofa bed where I had been sleeping for the last four nights. I sat there frozen, watching the frenzy in front of me. The world around me blurred and looked unreal. I felt detached and weightless, as if I were outside my own body.

A massive oxygen tank was wheeled in. Nurses fumbled with the tubes, attaching them to Bhanu's nose. The room was filled with urgent whispers, quick movements, hushed talks, worried glances exchanged over beeping monitors.

One nurse shook her head.

Then the ward doctor and the head nurse came in, a piece of paper in hand.

"Your husband's lungs and chest are filled with mucus," the doctor explained. "The oxygen isn't reaching his lungs. He cannot breathe. If this continues, he won't last long. We need to intubate him. We need your consent."

I have no idea what intubation truly meant. No one explained it to me. I only knew that it would help Bhanu breathe. It would keep him alive.

Like a robot, I signed the paper.

What happened next will haunt me forever.

I did not know how painful intubation was until I saw Bhanu fought it with everything he had. His frail arms flailed widely as the tubes were inserted into his nose and throat. Weak as he was, he struggled desperately to pull them out.

Then he let out a deafening cry, a sound of someone being tortured. A sound I had never heard before. A sound I would never forget. It was the first, and last, time I ever heard him cry out in pain.

I held his hand tightly. Lost in a world of unimaginable pain, he no longer recognized me. He struggled. He thrashed. He fought. He fought so hard that the nurses had to restrain his wrists, tying them to the bed.

Mercifully, the nurses sedated him.

"We cannot keep him in this room," the head nurse told me. "It is not equipped to monitor his condition. We have to move him to the ICU ward. It's like an ICU, but there are multiple patients in an open hall rather than private rooms."

I nodded numbly, watching as they wheeled Bhanu out of the suite.

And then I was alone.

I sat there, paralyzed, my mind struggling to process what had just happened. How had the morning begun with breakfast and ended like this? I could not believe it. I would not believe it.

No, he will get better. He will not leave me. Not yet.

I tried to ignore a voice deep inside me whispering the truth. He is at death's door.

A wave of guilt crashed over me.

It was my fault. I should not have given him that milk. I should not have transferred him to this hospital.

I could still see Bhanu struggling. Still heard his cry of pain. It echoed through my mind. Relentless, unforgiving.

And I knew with sickening certainty that nothing would never be the same again.

The ICU Ward

The head nurse returned after some time. Her face grave, her voice gentle as she led me to the ICU ward.

Patients lay everywhere. Their beds crammed together with barely any space between them. Families huddled close to their loved ones, squeezed into whatever space they could find.

Despite the crowding, the ward was eerily silent. Conversations were hushed, voices thick with sorrow as people waited stoically for the inevitable.

Then, I saw Bhanu, heavily sedated but his face still bore the signs of the trauma he had just endured. A tube ran through his nose, another protruded from his slightly twisted open mouth. Wires and monitors surrounded him, quietly displaying his vital signs.

His heart rate was abnormally high but his respiration rate and blood pressure remained stable. His oxygen level had returned to 100 per cent.

The attending physician approached me.

"It is my fault," I said, my voice trembling, as guilt filled my chest. "I gave him that milk."

The doctor looked at me with quiet sympathy. "Do not blame yourself," he said. "Your husband has pneumonia. It could have happened anytime."

Then after a pause, he continued. "Your husband is very sick. His cancer has spread. If his heart stops suddenly, you may want to consider not resuscitating him."

I knew what he was trying to say but would not. There is no point in resuscitating him. He will die anyway.

I realized then why he was telling me this. He wanted me to sign the DNR (Do Not Resuscitate). He wanted me to agree to let Bhanu go.

The doctor continued, explaining the rationale behind it. He spoke of pain, of broken bones, of the trauma resuscitation would inflict on Bhanu's already fragile body.

"If his heart stops, we'll make sure he does not feel anything. We'll give him all the necessary medication to keep him comfortable."

I was not listening to the doctor. His words were full of contradictions. My mind was elsewhere, trapped in the recent past. Just a few hours ago, Bhanu had smiled at me. A few minutes before that, he had apologized for keeping me awake all night.

He had been worried about *me*, not about his failing health, not his clogged throat, not how tired he was for lack of sleep. Not the pain from cancer that had been attacking him almost incessantly.

And now this doctor is telling me to let him go.

My heart broke. I could not sign the DNR.

But my son and Bhanu's elder brother did.

"Your husband is heavily sedated, but he can hear you," the doctor said.

"Really? If he is heavily sedated, how could he hear me?", I wanted to argue.

But I was too exhausted, physically, emotionally, in every way possible.

How could I talk to him with all these people around? There was no privacy. I had a thousand things I wanted to tell him, but the moment would not allow it.

Nurses and doctors moved efficiently through the ward, tending to patients. Some patients were being transferred out, maybe their condition had improved. Or, maybe someone had stopped breathing. It was a well-managed chaos, carried out in silence.

Bhanu's friend, Noi, came together with a few of his former colleagues from TU. They spoke to him briefly, offering quiet words of comfort. With no expected changes in Bhanu's condition for the rest of the afternoon, we left.

"We'll notify you if his condition worsens," the doctor said. "Usually, we contact the patient's family about two hours before they pass."

The head nurse told me I needed to vacate Bhanu's suite as another patient needed the room.

I returned to the silent suite, methodically gathering Bhanu's things. His mobile phone. The unused adult diapers. The remaining skin lotion he liked me to apply to his arms and legs. The medications he no longer needed.

I packed his shoes, his socks, the trousers and shirt he wore on the way to this hospital, clothes that I had not even had time to wash. Only six days ago, I thought. Just six days ago.

Everything had happened so fast. I had hoped he would continue his treatment here. That he would eat more. That he would look happier. That he would feel hopeful.

Then I saw it, his dark olive-green sweater. The one I had bought for him in December. He had worn it every day since. Even when the weather was warm, he felt cold. As I placed it into the suitcase among his other things, my tears started to fall.

Outside, we waited for a taxi.

"I think it would be impossible for us to reach TU hospital in two hours if you stay in our condo," my son said.

I nodded, fighting back tears. "Alright, I am going to stay at our house in Muang Ake. It is only about 20 minutes from here," I said.

And with that, we left.

Pulmonary ICU

The next morning my son called to tell me that Bhanu had been moved to the Pulmonary ICU. I rushed to the hospital.

When I arrived at Thammasat, its grounds were awash with color from hundreds of flowering trees, now heavy with yellow and orange blossoms, the colors of the university. In the gardens, bougainvilleas were bursting in red, orange, white, pink, and yellow.

April has arrived, bringing with it blinding sunlight and scorching heat. But as I stepped inside the hospital, the world outside faded. Here, everything was white, cold, sterile.

Admittance to the Pulmonary ICU was highly regulated. Anyone visiting a patient had to be disinfected against the Covid-19 virus before entering.

The Pulmonary ICU was pristine, its wall an unbroken white. The air was chilly, aseptic. There were eight rooms in the L-shaped ICU unit with the nurses' station in the center. Bhanu's room, Number 8, was farthest from the entrance.

Silently, nervously, I stepped inside.

Bhanu was still heavily sedated. His arms were tied to the bed to prevent him from pulling out the tubes if he woke up. Wires and machines surrounded him, an IV feeding him antibiotics, morphine and liquid food, and the vital signs monitor.

He was hooked to monitors. Their quiet beeping filled the room. Aside from his elevated heart rate, his vitals were stable. His oxygen level had returned to 100 per cent. His breathing and blood pressure were within normal range.

On the surface, everything seemed under control.

He looked different, marked by suffering. A tube ran through his nose. Another came from his mouth, which hung open as if in silent protest. His face was drawn with pain, as though even in unconsciousness, his body remembered the trauma of intubation. The machines kept him breathing, the morphine kept him from suffering.

A nurse brought me a chair. I sat beside him and took his hands. They were warm. I closed my eyes and imagined the blood flowing through his veins, carrying oxygen to his heart, keeping him alive.

I clasped his hands tightly, willing him to feel my presence.

Softly, I began to pray the rosary, my tears falling silently.

I sat there for hours. Holding his hand. Watching. Listening to the quiet hum of the machines and the occasional beeping of the vitals monitor.

I did not want to leave him alone in this cold, sterile place with only these machines keeping him company. I knew he would want me to stay. But I have no choice. Reluctantly, I left, returning to an empty house.

This was my new daily routine.

On the third day I asked the ICU doctor how Bhanu was doing. Quietly, she motioned me to step out of the room.

"He still has pneumonia, but we are seeing some improvement," she said. Then she hesitated.

I felt my stomach drop before she even spoke again.

"There is another problem," she continued "He has fungal infection in his bloodstream," she paused, letting her words settle. "We are treating him with antifungal medication. It will take another fourteen days."

Do Not Resuscitate

A few minutes later, I was called to a small conference room to meet the palliative care team. They were young, too young. All of them were doctors in their mid-20s. Their eyes were kind, their voices gentle. The leader, a male doctor, motioned me to sit.

I felt like a lamb to the slaughter.

The soft voices, the sympathetic glances, the careful preliminaries .... I sat there, waiting for the coup de grace. My heart pounded.

"Please sit down, Madam," the leader started.

"As you know, your husband has cancer." (*Yes, I know that very well. I have been taking care of him for the last 16 weeks.*)

"The cancer has spread to his other organs." (*I know that already.*)

"His cancer treatment is now suspended... (*You mean stopped.*)

"... because he is too weak to receive chemotherapy." (*I know that already. What do you want to tell me?*) I wanted to scream.

The doctor's voice shifted, losing its softness. "His vitals are still stable, but there may come a time when his blood pressure drops dangerously low. This could lead to shock, and eventual death."

He exhaled. The final blow was coming.

"Given the progression of his cancer, you may want to consider signing a consent to withhold any further medical intervention - no more medication, no mechanical aid to stabilize his blood pressure."

There it was. The same message the ICU Ward doctor had given me four days ago.

But I could not even begin to consider letting Bhanu die. How could I? How would I go on in this world without him? The thought was unbearable.

So, I played the religion card.

"I am Catholic. In my faith, we let God decide how long we live. We keep people alive for years, even if they are in a coma."

The doctors glanced at one another. Their young faces looked uneasy. (Maybe they were thinking that they could not be treating this elderly person for months and years. Maybe they wanted to do something else, something more challenging).

The leader hesitated, then spoke again. "How is your relationship with your son?

I blinked. "What?"

"I asked him if he knew why your husband is fighting so hard to live. He thinks… your husband is very worried about you. That nobody will take care of you when he is gone."

There in the sterile, cold room, I lost it.

"We'll let you think about the consent," the doctor said quietly, signaling the end of the meeting.

That evening, our son signed the consent.

Quality of Life

The following day, another group of Palliative Care team visited Bhanu. Outside his room, the leader, a 30-something woman talked to me.

"You should consider your husband's quality of life," she said.

"Meaning?" I asked.

"Perhaps it is time to consider removing his tubes to improve his quality of life," her voice was devoid of any emotion.

I had read earlier that most patients usually die within minutes after extubating.

"If we remove the tubes, he will die. So, there is no quality of life, because he is dead," I snapped.

I looked at the eager, well-trained, young faces of the Palliative Care team. They knew about medicine, but they knew nothing about life.

Bhanu had not been here more than a week, and already they were ready to let him go, I thought.

The team leader continued her well-rehearsed speech, explaining why I should consider taking Bhanu off life support.

"Why can't we just let nature take its course?" I shot back. "Besides, I do not want to play God! I can't. I won't." My voice trembled with emotion.

"Why don't we ask my husband what he wants? He is not comatose, just heavily sedated!" I argued. "You could wake him up."

After consulting with her team and other doctors (oncology, internal medicine), the Palliative Care team leader agreed to reduce Bhanu's sedation, to wake him.

The Will to Live

Two days later, Bhanu opened his eyes. He was mildly sedated, his arms still tied to the bed.

"He tried to write something, but his handwriting was unreadable," the ICU doctor told me.

As was my habit now, I scanned the vitals monitor the moment I entered the room. His heart rate was still slightly above normal. His heart was strong. I exhaled in relief.

That morning, Bhanu's friend, Noi, was with me when the doctor said, "We don't know how he can communicate with us."

"I'll tell him to blink," I replied. It was a technique I remembered from the book *The Diving Bell and the Butterfly* (original French title, *Le Scaphandre et le Papillon*) by Jean-Dominique Bauby.

I took Bhanu's hand. His gaze met mine.

Gently, slowly but loud enough for him to hear and understand, I said, "Darling, I will ask you some questions. Blink twice for yes, once for no. Do you understand?"

Bhanu blinked twice. I smiled.

I hesitated before I asked the next question, my stomach twisting. "Do you want to remove the tubes?" I asked nervously, fearful of what he would reply.

Bhanu blinked twice. My heart skipped a beat.

"Darling," I whispered, "if the tubes are removed, you won't survive. You will die," I said, fighting hard to keep my voice from breaking. "Would you still like to remove the tubes?" My heart pounded as I waited.

Bhanu searched my face.

Did he see the anguish in my eyes? Did he hear the silent cries of my heart? Perhaps he felt what I felt. "I do not want you to go! I can't bear to lose you! I know you are suffering, but please, stay with me a little longer!"

Or, was he thinking "I'm not giving up! I will fight. I can't leave you. Who will take care of you if I go?"

Whatever his reason, he did not blink. Instead, he closed his eyes and pretended to sleep.

I clasped his hands, my eyes burning with unshed tears. Still holding on to each other, I prayed the rosary. With each prayer, Bhanu squeezed my thumb.

For the following days, I visited Bhanu daily -- weekends, holidays, even during the Buddhist New Year when the hospital was nearly empty. I had become such a fixture that the cleaning ladies and some nurses assumed I was an out-patient in physiotherapy.

Anesthesia ICU - Remembering Ueno Park

By the second week of Bhanu's confinement in the Pulmonary ICU, a surge of Covid-19 patients filled the unit, forcing his transfer to the nearly empty Anesthesia ICU.

This unit was larger but less immaculate, less structured. Unlike the Pulmonary ICU, where the nurse's station was enclosed by a glass wall, here it was open, accessible. Bhanu's room was tucked at the farthest corner, away from the entrance.

When I sat beside him, my gaze drifted upward. A painting of a flower garden in vivid colors covered the ceiling. There were green trees and grass, and red, pink and yellow flowers blooming beneath a bright, blue sky. It was beautiful, but it was not real. And yet, it pulled me back to another garden, one we walked through together.

On our last trip to Japan, we wandered through Ueno Park, hoping to catch the last cherry blossoms. It was mid-April, and nearly all the cherry blossoms had fallen. Only one tree still held its blossoms, its petals dropping steadily to the ground.

But any disappointment faded as we strolled deeper through the park, where 600 peonies, known as "King of the Hundred Flowers", bloomed in brilliant shades of yellow, pink, white, and red. Bleeding hearts, rhododendron, and wisteria tumbled around in wild abundance.

I remembered Bhanu pausing under the last cherry tree, catching a petal in his hand, smiling as the wind carried it away.

We were supposed to return this spring, to walk together once more in that sea of flowers. Instead, he lay motionless in this cold, windowless, colorless ICU, fighting for his life.

Family Visit

After nearly three weeks alone, my elder sister, Teresita, and her daughter, Grace, joined me from the Philippines. Their arrival made my life a lot better. Now, I have someone to talk to, someone to be with me at night, someone to cook my meals.

My mother used to say that among her six children, Teresita -- who we all called Ateng -- was the only one she could always count on in times of need. How right she was.

Ateng and Grace accompanied me on my next visit to Bhanu. When we entered his room, he was asleep, sedated once again. The nurses had increased his sedation. He had become too restless, too agitated. Machines hummed softly around him, their beeping the only sound in the forlorn ICU.

By now, the Palliative Care team had become gentler in their approach, providing weekly update on Bhanu's condition, their voices softer, their words more careful.

"I noticed that his heart rate went up when he heard you," Ateng said, glancing at the monitor. There was a note of encouragement in her voice.

I looked at the monitor. His heart rate was still high. "He is still fighting," I thought. But then I looked at his face. His mouth was slightly open as he lay unconscious. Is he in pain? How uncomfortable must he feel. These thoughts gnawed at me.

The three of us stood by his bedside and prayed the rosary. I clung to the familiar rhythm of the words, finding comfort in them. *"When two or three are gathered in my name, there am I among them." (Matthew 18.20).*

The following day, a Catholic priest, Father Augustin from the Xaverian Missionaries, joined us in our prayers. We prayed for Bhanu. We prayed for me. For wisdom. For courage. For strength to do what was right.

Chapter Six
May: Journey to the Stars

"When he shall die,
Take him and cut him out in little stars,
And he will make the face of heaven so fine
That all the world will be in love with night
And pay no worship to the garish sun."
- William Shakespeare, "Romeo and Juliet"

Organs Began to Fail

It was the 25th of April. Bhanu had been in ICU for three weeks now.

I was on my daily visit that day when the ICU nurse told me that the internal medicine doctor wanted to talk to me. The words sent a chill through me. Something was wrong.

But when I entered Bhanu's room, his vitals were normal. His heart rate hovered around 100, steady, strong. He was still sedated.

Then the doctor arrived. She asked me to step outside. I followed her into the nurses' station, dreading what she was about to say.

There she told me something I prayed I would not hear.

"Your husband's organs have started to fail. I'm sorry," she said, her expression blank.

Inside, my heart was breaking.

I turned back toward the room, toward the vitals monitor, as if it might contradict her. His numbers were stable. His heart was still beating: steady, insistent, strong, as if he was healthy.

I clung to that. He can't be dying. Not yet.

Somehow, I found the courage to ask the unthinkable. "How much time does he have?"

The doctor hesitated. "About a week. It is hard to be definite."

A week.

She continued, "We have to stop feeding him. His digestive system won't be able to process food anymore. It will cause more discomfort."

I swallowed hard. Would he feel hungry? Would he suffer more?

The doctor seemed to sense my thoughts. "We'll give him medication to make sure he won't feel anything."

I nodded numbly.

Then she added, "I don't know if he can still feel touch. But he can still hear."

I returned to Bhanu's side, and sat beside him, taking his hand. It was warm. I let it rest on my functioning right hand, letting its weight settle there. His hand was heavy. He gripped my hand weakly, barely noticeable, but I thought maybe he was still fighting. Or maybe I was only imagining it.

I looked at the painting on the ceiling -- the flower garden. Once again, I was back in Ueno Park. Bhanu was holding my hand, just like he always did, guiding me through the narrow spaces between the endless rows of spring flowers.

He always held my hand. Always, even when we slept.

I wanted to stay by his side forever. I knew our time was slipping away, yet foolishly, I still wished for a thousand more days. A thousand more nights of holding his hand.

I could visit him anytime, stay as long as I wanted, but eventually, I had to go home. By the time I left, the sun had already set.

Taxis were scarce and even the ride-sharing cars were difficult to find. I waited for nearly an hour before finally getting a ride. The driver glanced at my walking stick.

"I hope you're better," he said kindly.

I swallowed hard, his simple concern unraveling me. My voice was unsteady when I replied. "I am not a patient. It's my husband. He has cancer."

My tears came before I could stop them.

The driver did not say anything. The rest of the ride was silent.

By the time we reached home, the night had fully settled in.

As I stepped out of the car, the driver spoke again, his voice gentle. "Be careful."

I nodded, unsteady on my feet, stepping into the darkness.

Music and Memories

The following day, a group of Bhanu's colleagues and former students came to visit. I did not tell them that his organs had started to fail.

Because of the life support machines, his vitals appeared normal. His heart rate, fluctuating between 95 and 100, was still slightly higher than average.

"He's still fighting," I thought, caught between unrealistic hope and creeping defeat.

"He's sedated," I told them. "But he wakes up from time to time. And he can hear if you speak near him."

One by one, they stepped forward.

"Fight, Ajarn! Fight! We are all praying for you to get well," each one said, their voices filled with quiet urgency.

Then, one former student suggested, "We should let him listen to music."

Music! Why hadn't I thought of it before? Bhanu loved music. It had always been a part of our lives. It would keep him company while he lay alone in the ICU at night.

Music had been the bridge that first connected us. When we first met, we quickly discovered our shared love of classical music and other genres.

The first event we ever attended as a couple was a violin recital at the University of the Philippines Los Banos auditorium. That night, we sat side by side, listening to pieces by Lalo, Sarasate and Schubert's deeply romantic and melancholic *Serenade*.

It was the beginning of our lifelong pastime -- sitting next to each other, listening to music, mostly classical but also movie themes and songs of artists like the Beatles, the Bee Gees, and many others that shaped our youth in the 1970s.

One of his former students volunteered, "We will prepare a recording of music and bring it here tomorrow."

I did not want to wait. I wanted Bhanu to listen to music now. I took out my phone and tried playing something on YouTube. But there was no internet connection in the ICU.

Determined, Ateng, Grace and I rushed to the nearest shopping mall to buy anything that could play or record music, a tape recorder, a Walkman, an iPod. But they were obsolete; nobody sold them anymore.

Dejected, we all went home. But I was not giving up.

That evening, before Grace left for Manila, we found another way. My phone had a voice recorder and at home, we still have an old CD/radio player.

Before she left for the airport, we recorded Beethoven's *Sonata No. 14 in C major*, the *Moonlight Sonata*. I also recorded Bach's comforting *Prelude in C major* (the same piece that Charles Guonod would later use for his *Ave Maria*), Mozart's *Eine Kleine Nacht Musik* and *Adagio* from *Clarinet Concerto*. Pieces of music that Bhanu loved.

The next morning, I rushed to the ICU with the recordings. As the first notes of the hauntingly sad, nostalgic first notes of the *Moonlight Sonata* filled Bhanu's ICU room, he opened his eyes.

"Do you like the music, darling?" I asked him.

My heart swelled with joy when, for the first time in months, his eyes twinkled. And for the briefest moment, he smiled. His last.

As Bhanu and I listened to Beethoven's immortal music, I could not help but remember those nights in Baltimore when we would end our long days by listening to Karl Hass' classical music program on the radio.

The program's signature opening music was the *Adagio cantabile* of Beethoven's *Pathetique* (*Sonata Number 8 in C-minor*), a piece so calming it felt like a warm embrace at the end of a stressful day.

After *Moonlight Sonata*, we listened to Mozart's lively *Eine Kleine Nacht Musik*, and once again I was transported to our student days at Johns Hopkins.

Every weekend we watched free movies, including "*Amadeus*," at Shriver Hall. No matter the weather, rain or snow, the hall was packed with students looking for a break from academic rigor. The shows always started with the *Looney Tunes*, and for a few moments, we all became children, laughing at *Bugs Bunny* and *Tom and Jerry* before the main feature.

After the *Eine Kleine Nacht Musik*, we listened to Bach's *Prelude in C-Major*, a piece so angelic it seemed to lift the soul toward heaven.

Bach brought me back memories of our summers in Baltimore.

We had been young then, living in one of Johns Hopkins University's student apartments. I was taking summer classes at Towson University, a 30-minute bus ride from our apartment.

Summers in Baltimore were oppressively hot and we could not afford an air conditioner. While other foreign students were taking road trips, we could not afford to go anywhere outside Baltimore, except to Washington, DC.

We had little money, but we had each other.

Our favorite form of entertainment was watching "M*A*S*H" on our small black and white TV. One episode became particularly special for us, when Hawkeye Pierce advised Klinger to impress his pianist date by exclaiming, "Ah, Bach!"

From then on "Ah, Bach!" became our inside joke whenever we listened to his music.

As Schubert's *Ave Maria* played, we prayed the rosary together.

I prayed for Bhanu.

For a miracle.

"Please let him live a little longer. Let us grow old together."

"Grow old along with me…"

The first time I quoted those words to Bhanu was in one of our Wednesdays love letters when we were in Baltimore. On Wednesdays, we had different class schedules so we could not have lunch together.

Instead, we left notes for each other - small, loving, humorous messages left on the dining table, waiting to be read.

Decades later, Bhanu still quoted those words in my birthday cards.

Now, I sat beside him, holding his hand, and silently pleading with the universe for more time.

A Familiar Name

Bhanu had fallen asleep while we were praying, his hand still touching mine. Gently, I placed it on his side.

Then, I stood up to go out for lunch. As I stepped out of the ICU, I nearly bumped into a tall guy with a worried expression. He looked at me, hesitated, and then asked, "Are you here for Ajarn Bhanupong?"

"Yes," I replied.

"You must be his wife. I'm Phongton. Ton," he said.

I stared at him in surprise. "Ton! You are Ton. I'm so happy to finally meet you. Ajarn Bhanupong often spoke about you. I feel like I already know you," I said happily.

"I always visit him in the evenings," Ton explained. "That is why we haven't seen each other before."

Then softly, he asked, "How is he?"

Reluctantly, I told him the truth. "His organs have started to fail. The doctors said that he only has about a week. But he can still hear, for now."

"There is always hope," Ton said, offering me a quiet reassurance.

"I had recorded some music for him," I said. "I wish I could leave my phone with him so he could listen to music while he is alone."

Ton nodded, "I'd like to see him."

Together, we returned to Bhanu's room.

Ton placed his phone near Bhanu and played a recording of Chopin's *Nocturne Opus 9 No. 2 in E flat* and Tchaikovsky's *Violin Concerto in D major*, two of Bhanu's favorites.

"I'll record more for him," Ton promised.

Over the following days, I added more to our growing playlist: Shubert's *Serenade D 957*, Vivaldi's *Mandolin Concerto in C major* (one of the two records he bought for me on my 25th birthday. He knew I loved Italian Baroque music; the other was Mozart's *Piano Concerto No. 21 in C major).*

Then came the movie themes.

The tender and poignant second movement of Mozart's *Clarinet Concerto in A Major* from *Out of Africa*; the bittersweet *Pelagia's Song* from *Captain Corelli's Mandolin*; the evocative *Cavalleria Rusticana* from *The Godfather III*; the sweet, achingly sad theme from *Cinema Paradiso*, and the uplifting, prayer-like *Gabriel's Oboe* from *The Mission*.

These melodies were more than just music. They were echoes of a life spent together, of shared moments in darkened theaters, or in the comfort of our living room, of whispered commentary or brief argument, of laughter, and the warmth of his hand in mine.

And in those last days, as Bhanu lay in the ICU, most of his organs failing but his ears still listening, music carried him through, one melody at a time.

Hanging On

By the end of the first week when his organs started failing, Bhanu's condition was unchanged. His vitals remained normal, though he had grown quieter, more subdued. Asleep most of the time, his hands were no longer restrained.

As I had done every day in the past four weeks, I sat beside him, praying. Holding his hands for hours until it was time for me to leave. His hands were still warm.

When the first week ended, I exhaled in relief. I still had him. I still could visit him. I still could hold his hands, still feel the life within them. But how much longer? How many more days did we have left, to pray together, to listen to music, to simply be?

I studied his face. It is much thinner now, skeletal, with barely a trace of flesh left. His mouth, twisted slightly for being open for nearly a month, was a painful reminder of all he had endured.

And yet, I still could see the fight in his exhausted, tired eyes.

They were unfocused now, drifting between wakefulness and sleep, but every so often, a glint of strength would flicker in them-faint but unmistakable. As if some part of him still refused to let go.

As the second week progressed, Ton recorded more musical pieces on his phone, playing them for Bhanu as often as he could.

For the first half of the week, Bhanu's vitals remained stable. But then, at the end of the second week, everything changed.

A nurse met me at the entrance of the ICU, her expression unreadable.

"We almost called you early this morning," she said.

My heart pounded. My stomach tightened. "What happened?"

"Ajarn's blood pressure dropped suddenly from 110/75 to 75/52," she stated matter-of-factly.

I rushed, eyes darting to the vitals monitor.

The numbers had stabilized. His blood pressure now fluctuated between 110/75 and 95/70, low, but not yet at a critical level.

I hurried to his side, calling his name. As in the previous days, his heart rate spiked above 100 before settling back in the mid-90s. Still normal. But his eyes remained closed.

I reached for his right hand. It was not as warm as before.

Edema had set in. His hands were heavier; his heart was beginning to fail.

We prayed together, as we always did. But this time, something was different.

For weeks, Bhanu had always responded, however faintly. A slight squeeze of my fingers. A glimmer of acknowledgment. Now his fingers were limp on mine.

A knife sliced through my heart as I looked at his face.

It had been five weeks since he was intubated. Five weeks with his mouth forced open.

It had been two weeks since they stopped feeding him. His lips were parched and dry. The nurses sometimes applied petroleum jelly to moisten them, but it was never enough.

I prayed as I always did. But this time, I pleaded for mercy.

"Please God, let Bhanu's suffering end."

At the same time, I was not ready.

"Please, just a little longer."

The second week of organ failure ended with an ominous sign. His blood pressure was now dipping below normal.

It was early May.

The hot season was ending.

Still, Bhanu's heart kept beating.

I'll See You Among the Stars

The sky over Muang Ake was untouched by the smog that blanketed Bangkok.

One night, as I looked at the vast expanse of stars, a memory surfaced. One from long ago, during the early days of our courtship in Los Banos. We had been walking home on a night just like this, the stars shining over us.

At that time, Bhanu was preparing to return to Bangkok. "We might be thousands of miles apart," he said, squeezing my hand, "but we'll be looking at the same stars. So, when you miss me, just look at the stars. I will be looking at them, too, as if I'm right next to you."

But tonight, Bhanu was alone in the ICU.

He could no longer look at the stars.

He could hardly see.

Internal Medicine ICU

The next morning, Bhanu was transferred to the Internal Medicine ICU. It was a stark change from the previous two ICUs, where he had been confined within four sterile walls, where the world outside barely existed.

This time his room had a large window. Sunlight poured in, bathing the space in warmth, filling it with an atmosphere of hope, of life.

"Bhanu has not seen the sun or the blue sky for more than a month," I thought. "I hope he can see them now."

Outside his room, I asked to speak with the attending physician.

He was young with curly hair and bespectacled. His voice was clipped, impatient.

"What is the point of keeping him alive?" he asked, looking at me with thinly veiled irritation.

I froze.

The words hit me like a slap.

How dare he?

I stared at this child of a doctor, my grief turning into anger.

Does he have parents? Has he ever loved someone that losing them was unthinkable? Does he know what it is to watch the person you love most in this world slowly slipping away?

I forced myself to speak.

"Is he comatose?"

"No."

"Can he still feel?" I asked.

The doctor shrugged, "I don't know."

"Can he still hear?"

"I don't know," he repeated, curt and dismissive.

Then, impatiently, he added: "Do you have any other questions?"

My hands trembled. My voice turned sharp, cutting the sterile air. My temper got the better of me.

"No," I snapped. "Because you don't seem to know anything."

Then, I turned and walked into Bhanu's room. I stood beside him, taking his hands in mine. I massaged his arms gently.

The nurse told me that he was asleep but his eyes remained open. He could not close them.

I caressed his sunken cheeks, so thin they felt like they could tear, delicate as paper.

The nurse, seeing my anguish, silently offered me a chair. I sat down and prayed the rosary, holding his hand. They were cold.

"Please, dear Virgin Mary, please dear Lord, have mercy on my husband."

Gabriel's Oboe played softly from Ton's recording, its prayerful melody drifting through the room, mingling with the golden light filtering through the window.

The next day was Friday.

As my taxi entered Thammasat's sprawling campus, I noticed the flame trees. Their petals had fallen to the ground. One by one, the wind carried them away.

Once so vibrant, now they laid to waste by the fickle cruelty of nature. Soon, they would vanish from the earth.

The hospital was quiet that morning.

After paying the hospital's weekly charges, I hurried upstairs to see Bhanu.

As I entered his room, the nurse met my gaze. "His blood pressure is very low," she said. Then she turned and walked away, avoiding my questions.

I looked at the vitals monitor. His blood pressure plummeted to 70/52, then 65/50.

Dangerously low.

But his heart rate was still fluctuating between 100 and 90.

I leaned close.

"Darling, I'm here," I whispered.

No flicker. No response.

Only a tiny blip on the monitor, a faint reaction in his heart rate.

I studied his face. There were scratches around his open eyes. The pupils had disappeared, leaving only white.

I stroked his arms. They were covered once again; he must have been agitated earlier.

Then I prayed the rosary. My fingers wrapped around his wrist.

My teeth began to chatter. A sudden, creeping cold filled the room.

I sat beside him for hours, watching him as the sunlight dimmed, giving way to the encroaching darkness.

Before I left, as I had done for nearly three weeks, I leaned close to Bhanu and paraphrased the words from *The Letter of Saint Paul to Timothy*:

"You have fought the good fight, you have won the race, you have kept the faith."

And then quoted the lines by E.E. Cummings:

"Yours is the light by which my spirit is born,
Yours is the darkness of my soul's return
You are my sun, my moon, and all my stars."

As I left Bhanu that late afternoon, Elgar's *Salut d'Amour* played softly in the background, a tender melody of deep love and devotion.

The last rays of the sun filtered through the window, casting long shadows across the room.

Outside, the hot, bright, colorful summer days were coming to an end.

On my way home, it rained.

By the time the taxi pulled onto the main road, the storm began in earnest. Raindrops pelted the windshield, blurring the streetlights in a hazy glow.

The rhythmic tapping of water against glass filled the silence inside the cab, matching the heaviness in my heart.

As I watched the rain veil the city, another night, long ago, came rushing back.

Suddenly, I was in Baltimore again. It was spring 1983.

I was pursuing my MBA at the University of Baltimore, while Bhanu was finishing his PhD in economics at Johns Hopkins University.

The day's forecast had promised light evening rain with temperatures hovering in the low 40s. Nothing unusual. But by midday the sky darkened and the temperature plummeted. By late afternoon, snow flurries danced in the air, turning into full-fledged storm.

By the time my 6 p.m. class began, the city was blanketed in white. Public buses had stopped running, the roads became impassable, and visibility plummeted.

Across town, Bhanu sat in front of a computer lost in his dissertation. Computers, back then, were massive machines housed in computer laboratories. As he made his way to our apartment, concern for me weighed heavily on Bhanu's mind.

Was my class canceled? Had I made home safely? Was I out in the cold without shelter?

I was wearing only a pullover and a light jacket that day. So, he hastily grabbed my winter coat and set off on foot.

For nearly three miles, he walked through the biting wind and falling snow, the icy air slicing through his jacket. His hands trembled from the cold, but he kept going.

More than an hour later, he arrived.

He found me sitting in the university cafeteria, sipping warm, overly sweet chocolate. Relief flooded his face as he handed me my coat.

"Come," he said, slipping his freezing fingers around mine.

Arm in arm we crossed the snowy North Charles Street and made our way to the Johns Hopkins shuttle bus waiting to transport students returning from the School of Advanced International Studies in

Washington, DC to Homewood campus. The bus was warm, the windows fogged from conversations and body heat. We sat in comfortable silence, his hand still holding mine.

Decades had passed since that night, but Bhanu had never changed. He had always been the man who would walk three miles in a snowstorm just to make sure I was safe.

Now, he was alone in the ICU, still fighting to live, to be there for me.

As the rain kept falling, I blinked, the past dissolving. Then through watery haze, I saw the light at the gate bathed in rain. Home.

The taxi slowed, tires crunching on the wet pavement.

Then the phone rang.

A Jesuit priest was calling me.

We spoke about Bhanu's condition. He told me the Catholic Church allows the removal of life support system if three conditions were met:

1. The patient is terminally ill with no chance of recovery. (Yes)
2. The patient has become a burden to the family financially and emotionally. (Financially, no. The university was subsidizing his hospital care. Emotionally, yes. It was unbearable to watch him suffer.)

3.   Even if the patient survives, he or she may never recover or live a meaningful life. (Nobody knew.)

At the end of the conversation, the priest gently advised, "Perhaps it is time to let him go."

That night, I prayed for guidance.

Then I sent a message to my son.

"If your father's condition is unchanged by the end of the month, we have to decide."

But in my heart, I begged Bhanu to help me.

"Darling, I can't do it. I could never consent to removing your life support. I don't mind visiting you every day for the rest of my life just to hold your hand. Just to be with you. But my heart feels shattered seeing your pain. I don't know what to do. Please help me."

Tears streamed down my cheeks as I thought of Bhanu. His suffering etched all over his hollowed face, like a road map of the peaks and valleys of the pain he went through for the last six months.

And still, he fought. Even when his blood pressure fell, his heart rate rose.

Then his words came back to me.

"I'm not afraid of dying. But I'm worried about you. I'm supposed to take care of you always."

So, he held on, for me.

For as long as he could.

At 9:45 the next morning, Bhanu's heart gave one last, fragile beat.

Then it stopped.

And with that final heartbeat, he made a choice I could never make.

He set me free.

And he began his journey to the stars.

The End

REFERENCES

The following quotations have been included in this memoir not only for their literary significance, but because they were deeply meaningful to both my husband and me. These lines reflect the thoughts, values, and shared moments that shaped our life together. They are among our favorite passages—words we turned to for comfort, insight, and reflection throughout our journey.

Jean-Dominique Bauby, *The Diving Bell and the Butterfly*

Although no direct quotations are used, the method of communication described in this memoir—developed between Bauby and his speech therapist—inspired the way I communicated with my husband when he was intubated. This extraordinary book offered both guidance and solace during that time.

—Translated from the French by Jeremy Leggatt, *Vintage International*, Vintage Books, A Division of Random House, Inc., New York, First Vintage International Edition, July 1998, Copyright 1997 by Editions Robert Laffont, S.A. Paris.

Robert Browning

"Grow old along with me! The best is yet to be…"

— From the poem, "Rabbi Ben Ezra." *Public domain.*

Emily Dickinson

"Because I could not stop for Death – He kindly

stopped for me –"

---From the poem "Because I Could not Stop for Death." *Public domain.*

"Hope is the thing with feathers-

That perches in the soul -

And sings the tune without the words -

And never stops - at all."

--From the poem "Hope is the Thing with Feathers." *Public domain.*

"Hope is a strange invention -

A Patent of the Heart-

In unremitting action.

Yet never wearing out."

---From the poem "Hope is a Strange Invention." *Public domain.*

Ecclesiastes 3:1

"There is an appointed time for everything, and a time for every purpose under the heavens…"

— *The Holy Bible*, Book of Ecclesiastes. *Public domain.*

E.E. Cummings

"Yours is the light by which my spirit is born,

Yours is the darkness of my soul's return

You are my sun, my moon, and all my stars."

---from poem #38, *Collected Poems: 1904-1962.*

Public domain.

Max Ehrmann

"Nurture strength of spirit to shield you in sudden misfortune. But do not distress yourself with dark imaginings. Many fears are born of fatigue and loneliness."

— From "Desiderata", attributed to Max Ehrmann. Quoted with appreciation.

Antoine de Saint-Exupéry

"Now here is my secret, very simply: you can only see things clearly with your heart. What is essential is invisible to the eye."

"For you, my star will just be one of the many. That way, you will love watching all of them."

"You become responsible, forever, for what you have tamed."

— From *The Little Prince (Le Petit Prince)*, First published as *Le Petit Prince* and simultaneously in English translation by Reynal and Hitchcock. 1943.

-Letter to a Hostage (*Lettre a un otage)*, was first published in French in 1943; the first English edition was published by Brentano's in the same year.

The above quotes are from translations by T. V. F. Cuffe, first published by Penguin Books, 1995; reprinted with color illustrations in 1998 by Penguin Group.

Thomas Gray

"Now fades the glimmering landscape on the sight

And all the air a solemn stillness holds."

---From the poem, "Elegy Written in a Country Churchyard." *Public domain.*

Saint Matthew

"When two or three are gathered in my name, there am I among them."

----*The Holy Bible,* Gospel of Matthew 18.20. *Public domain.*

Saint Paul

"I have fought the good fight, I have won the race, I have kept the faith."

---Letter of Saint Paul to Timothy 2 Timothy 4:7. *The Holy Bible. Public domain.*

William Shakespeare

"When he shall die,

Take him and cut him out in little stars,

And he will make the face of heaven so fine

That all the world will be in love with night

And pay no worship to the garish sun."

— From the play "*Romeo and Juliet*", *Act III, Scene* 2. *Public domain.*

Alfred, Lord Tennyson

"Behold, we know not anything;

I can but trust that good shall fall

At last—far off—at last, to all,

And every winter change to spring."

—From the poem *"In Memoriam A.H.H., Canto LIV." Public domain.*

Dylan Thomas

"Though wise men at their end know dark is right,

Because their words had forked no lightning they

Do not go gentle into that good night."

---From the poem, "Do Not Go Gentle into That Good Night." *Public domain.*

Hotel da Yama

I used the information on Hotel da Yama when I described our 40th anniversary celebration in Hakone, Japan.

https://www.hakone-hoteldeyama.jp/en/

These excerpts and references are used in accordance with fair use and are respectfully credited.

About the Author

Divina Blanco

Born in the Philippines, Divina is a retired corporate banker and climate finance specialist. Writing is her hobby. She has published a children's book, *Fugly Becomes Beauty* in 2022. She was married to Bhanupong Nidhiprabha, a professor of economics and former Dean of the Faculty of Economics, Thammasat University, Thailand.

www.ingramcontent.com/pod-product-compliance
Lightning Source LLC
LaVergne TN
LVHW041942070526
838199LV00051BA/2879